CURRICULUM COLLECTION

INTRODUCING ISSUES WITH OPPOSING VIEWPOINTS®

# Iran

Jennifer L. Skancke and Lauri S. Friedman, *Book Editors*

**GREENHAVEN PRESS**
*A part of Gale, Cengage Learning*

GALE CENGAGE Learning

Detroit • New York • San Francisco • New Haven, Conn • Waterville, Maine • London

Christine Nasso, *Publisher*
Elizabeth Des Chenes, *Managing Editor*

© 2010 Greenhaven Press, a part of Gale, Cengage Learning

Gale and Greenhaven Press are registered trademarks used herein under license.

*For more information, contact:*
Greenhaven Press
27500 Drake Rd.
Farmington Hills, MI 48331-3535
Or you can visit our Internet site at gale.cengage.com

**ALL RIGHTS RESERVED.**
No part of this work covered by the copyright herein may be reproduced, transmitted, stored, or used in any form or by any means graphic, electronic, or mechanical, including but not limited to photocopying, recording, scanning, digitizing, taping, Web distribution, information networks, or information storage and retrieval systems, except as permitted under Section 107 or 108 of the 1976 United States Copyright Act, without the prior written permission of the publisher.

For product information and technology assistance, contact us at

Gale Customer Support, 1-800-877-4253
For permission to use material from this text or product, submit all requests online at www.cengage.com/permissions

Further permissions questions can be e-mailed to permissionrequest@cengage.com

Articles in Greenhaven Press anthologies are often edited for length to meet page requirements. In addition, original titles of these works are changed to clearly present the main thesis and to explicitly indicate the author's opinion. Every effort is made to ensure that Greenhaven Press accurately reflects the original intent of the authors. Every effort has been made to trace the owners of copyrighted material.

Cover image Majid Saeedi/Getty Images.

---

**LIBRARY OF CONGRESS CATALOGING-IN-PUBLICATION DATA**

Iran / Jennifer L. Skancke and Lauri S. Friedman, book editors.
  p. cm. -- (Introducing issues with opposing viewpoints)
  Includes bibliographical references and index.
  ISBN 978-0-7377-4479-8 (hardcover)
  1. United States--Foreign relations--Iran. 2. Iran--Foreign relations--United States. 3. Iran--Politics and government--1997- 4. Iran--Military policy. 5. Weapons of mass destruction--Iran. 6. Iran--Foreign relations--Middle East. 7. Middle East--Foreign relations--Iran. I. Skancke, Jennifer. II. Friedman, Lauri S.
  E183.8.I55I736 2010
  327.73055--dc22
                                                                    2009024278

---

Printed in the United States of America
1 2 3 4 5 6 7 13 12 11 10 09

# Contents

Foreword     5
Introduction     7

## Chapter 1: How Dangerous Is the Threat from Iran?

1. Iran Poses a Serious Threat to the United States     11
   *Kenneth R. Timmerman*

2. Iran Does Not Pose a Serious Threat to the United States     20
   *Phyllis Bennis*

3. Iran Poses a Serious Threat to Israel     30
   *HonestReporting*

4. Iran Does Not Pose a Serious Threat to Israel     38
   *Leon Hadar*

5. Iran Poses a Threat to the Fragile Nation of Iraq     45
   *Jeffrey White*

6. Iran Is Not Likely to Help Terrorists Attack America and Its Allies     53
   *Ted Galen Carpenter*

## Chapter 2: Is Iran Developing Nuclear Weapons?

1. Iran Is Probably Developing Weapons of Mass Destruction     61
   *U.S. House of Representatives Permanent Select Committee on Intelligence, Subcommittee on Intelligence Policy*

2. Iran Is Probably Not Developing Nuclear Weapons     69
   *Juan Cole*

3. The United States Should Prevent Iran from Getting Nuclear Technology     76
   *American Israel Public Affairs Committee*

4. The United States Has No Right to Prevent Iran from Getting Nuclear Technology     84
   *S. Sam Shoamanesh*

# Chapter 3: How Should the United States Deal with Iran?

1. The United States Should Consider Declaring War on Iran     93
   *Peter Brookes*

2. The United States Should Not Consider Declaring War on Iran     98
   *Stephen Zunes*

3. The United States Should Impose Economic Sanctions on Iran     105
   *Daniel Doron*

4. The United States Should Initiate Talks with Iran     113
   *Reza Zia-Ebrahimi*

| | |
|---|---|
| Facts About Iran | 119 |
| Glossary | 123 |
| Organizations to Contact | 125 |
| For Further Reading | 130 |
| Index | 135 |
| Picture Credits | 140 |

# Foreword

Indulging in a wide spectrum of ideas, beliefs, and perspectives is a critical cornerstone of democracy. After all, it is often debates over differences of opinion, such as whether to legalize abortion, how to treat prisoners, or when to enact the death penalty, that shape our society and drive it forward. Such diversity of thought is frequently regarded as the hallmark of a healthy and civilized culture. As the Reverend Clifford Schutjer of the First Congregational Church in Mansfield, Ohio, declared in a 2001 sermon, "Surrounding oneself with only like-minded people, restricting what we listen to or read only to what we find agreeable is irresponsible. Refusing to entertain doubts once we make up our minds is a subtle but deadly form of arrogance." With this advice in mind, Introducing Issues with Opposing Viewpoints books aim to open readers' minds to the critically divergent views that comprise our world's most important debates.

Introducing Issues with Opposing Viewpoints simplifies for students the enormous and often overwhelming mass of material now available via print and electronic media. Collected in every volume is an array of opinions that captures the essence of a particular controversy or topic. Introducing Issues with Opposing Viewpoints books embody the spirit of nineteenth-century journalist Charles A. Dana's axiom: "Fight for your opinions, but do not believe that they contain the whole truth, or the only truth." Absorbing such contrasting opinions teaches students to analyze the strength of an argument and compare it to its opposition. From this process readers can inform and strengthen their own opinions, or be exposed to new information that will change their minds. Introducing Issues with Opposing Viewpoints is a mosaic of different voices. The authors are statesmen, pundits, academics, journalists, corporations, and ordinary people who have felt compelled to share their experiences and ideas in a public forum. Their words have been collected from newspapers, journals, books, speeches, interviews, and the Internet, the fastest growing body of opinionated material in the world.

Introducing Issues with Opposing Viewpoints shares many of the well-known features of its critically acclaimed parent series, Opposing Viewpoints. The articles are presented in a pro/con format, allowing readers to absorb divergent perspectives side by side. Active reading questions preface each viewpoint, requiring the student to approach the material thoughtfully and carefully. Useful charts, graphs, and cartoons supplement each article. A thorough introduction provides readers with crucial background on an issue. An annotated bibliography points the reader toward articles, books, and Web sites that contain additional information on the topic. An appendix of organizations to contact contains a wide variety of charities, nonprofit organizations, political groups, and private enterprises that each hold a position on the issue at hand. Finally, a comprehensive index allows readers to locate content quickly and efficiently.

Introducing Issues with Opposing Viewpoints is also significantly different from Opposing Viewpoints. As the series title implies, its presentation will help introduce students to the concept of opposing viewpoints and learn to use this material to aid in critical writing and debate. The series' four-color, accessible format makes the books attractive and inviting to readers of all levels. In addition, each viewpoint has been carefully edited to maximize a reader's understanding of the content. Short but thorough viewpoints capture the essence of an argument. A substantial, thought-provoking essay question placed at the end of each viewpoint asks the student to further investigate the issues raised in the viewpoint, compare and contrast two authors' arguments, or consider how one might go about forming an opinion on the topic at hand. Each viewpoint contains sidebars that include at-a-glance information and handy statistics. A Facts About section located in the back of the book further supplies students with relevant facts and figures.

Following in the tradition of the Opposing Viewpoints series, Greenhaven Press continues to provide readers with invaluable exposure to the controversial issues that shape our world. As John Stuart Mill once wrote: "The only way in which a human being can make some approach to knowing the whole of a subject is by hearing what can be said about it by persons of every variety of opinion and studying all modes in which it can be looked at by every character of mind. No wise man ever acquired his wisdom in any mode but this." It is to this principle that Introducing Issues with Opposing Viewpoints books are dedicated.

# Introduction

In 1979 Iran underwent a dramatic overhaul, the likes of which had never before been seen. In just a few short months, it was transformed from a pro-Western, antireligious, cosmopolitan nation into one that followed a strict version of Shia Islam. The new Islamic Republic of Iran adopted a repressive social code, one in which unrelated men and women are not allowed to walk together down the street, and where nail polish is regarded as a dangerous weapon. The Islamic Revolution of 1979 was led largely by young people who were fed up with the hypocrisy of their government. The revolution was staged on university campuses and populated by idealistic students who wanted to see their culture and religion play a larger role in their national lifestyle.

Thirty years later, the young people who led the Islamic Revolution are now in their fifties. But their children—a new generation of rebellious Iranians—have different ideas about how they want their country to be. This new generation did not participate in their parents' revolution—most of them were born in the 1980s, well after the tide of religious fervor swept through their country. Yet during the prime of their lives, when people tend to want the most social freedom, they have had to live under the social restrictions put in place by the revolution. As a result, Iran's young people are showing signs of being increasingly fed up with their repressive government—and could force significant change in that country as they demand the same things wanted by young people all over the world: freedom and fun.

As of 2009, nearly 70 percent of the Iranian population was under the age of thirty. Yet this massive group of young people has few avenues for enjoying their youth. Most forms of music are banned, as are dating and certain kinds of shopping. Many Web sites are censored or blocked by government officials, and alcohol is illegal. All of these restrictions are the result of the Islamic Revolution, but Iran's current crop of teenagers cares less about religion and more about being young. As Amir Shoja, a twenty-six-year-old Iranian who now lives in America, says, "Iranians my age don't want chadors [long, restrictive veils that cover the hands and head] and martyrs—they want CDs, cell phones, and nightclubs!"[1] Said another Iranian youth who lives

# Chapter 1

# How Dangerous Is the Threat from Iran?

*Iran's nuclear power plant at Bushehr is shown here. The facility is eight years behind schedule.*

Viewpoint 1

# Iran Poses a Serious Threat to the United States

## Kenneth R. Timmerman

"The United States [is] at risk of a sneak nuclear attack by a rogue nation or a terrorist group designed to take out our nation's critical infrastructure."

Kenneth R. Timmerman argues in the following viewpoint that Iran poses a serious threat to the United States. Timmerman explains that a congressionally established commission has warned that Iran has carried out missile tests for what could be a plan for a nuclear strike on the United States. The commission also warned that even a crude nuclear weapon produced by Iran could cripple military and civilian communications, power, transportation, water, food, and other infrastructure. Seventy to 90 percent of Americans might die or suffer if Iran carried out such an attack. Given Iran's anti-American sentiment and outright calls for the destruction of America, the author concludes it is critical for America to take the threat from Iran seriously.

A best-selling author, Timmerman is a contributing editor for Newsmax Media and has spent his career investigating the dark side of national security.

Kenneth R. Timmerman, "U.S. Intel: Iran Plans Nuclear Strike on U.S.," Newsmax.com, July 29, 2008. Copyright © 2008 Newsmax. All rights reserved. Reproduced by permission.

**AS YOU READ, CONSIDER THE FOLLOWING QUESTIONS:**
1. What is an EMP attack, and what effect does the author say it could have on the United States?
2. What would be the first indication of a direct nuclear strike on a U.S. city, according to Timmerman?
3. How does Barack Obama feel about a missile defense system, according to the author?

Iran has carried out missile tests for what could be a plan for a nuclear strike on the United States, the head of a national security panel has warned.

In testimony before the House Armed Services Committee and in remarks to a private conference on missile defense over the weekend hosted by the Claremont Institute, Dr. William Graham warned that the U.S. intelligence community "doesn't have a story" to explain the recent Iranian tests.

One group of tests that troubled Graham, the former White House science adviser under President Ronald Reagan, were successful efforts to launch a Scud missile from a platform in the Caspian Sea.

"They've got [test] ranges in Iran which are more than long enough to handle Scud launches and even Shahab-3 launches," Dr. Graham said. "Why would they be launching from the surface of the Caspian Sea? They obviously have not explained that to us."

Another troubling group of tests involved Shahab-3 launches where the Iranians "detonated the warhead near apogee [its highest point], not over the target area where the thing would eventually land, but at altitude," Graham said. "Why would they do that?"

Graham chairs the Commission to Assess the Threat to the United States from Electromagnetic Pulse (EMP) Attack, a blue-ribbon panel established by Congress in 2001.

The commission examined the Iranian tests "and without too much effort connected the dots," even though the U.S. intelligence community previously had failed to do so, Graham said.

"The only plausible explanation we can find is that the Iranians are figuring out how to launch a missile from a ship and get it up to altitude and then detonate it," he said. "And that's exactly what you would do if you had a nuclear weapon on a Scud or a Shahab-3 or other missile, and you wanted to explode it over the United States."

The commission warned in a report issued in April [2008] that the United States was at risk of a sneak nuclear attack by a rogue nation or a terrorist group designed to take out our nation's critical infrastructure.

"If even a crude nuclear weapon were detonated anywhere between 40 kilometers to 400 kilometers above the earth, in a split-second it would generate an electro-magnetic pulse that would cripple military and civilian communications, power, transportation, water, food, and other infrastructure," the report warned.

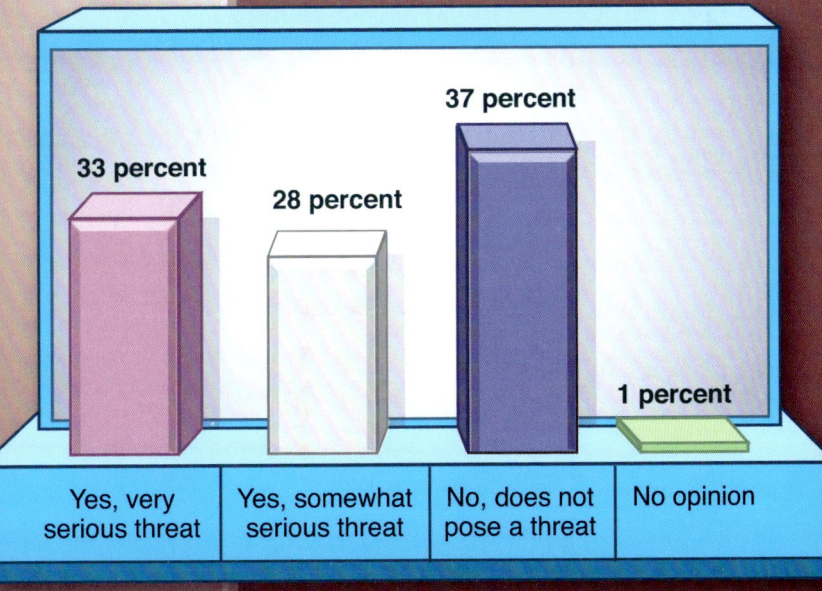

### Americans Are Worried About Iran

A 2007 Gallup poll found that 61 percent of Americans think Iran is either a "very serious" or a "somewhat serious" threat.

**Do you think Iran's nuclear program poses a serious threat to the United States, or not? Is that a very serious threat or a somewhat serious threat?**

- Yes, very serious threat: 33 percent
- Yes, somewhat serious threat: 28 percent
- No, does not pose a threat: 37 percent
- No opinion: 1 percent

Taken from: Gallup Poll, December 10–13, 2007.

While not causing immediate civilian casualties, the near-term impact on U.S. society would dwarf the damage of a direct nuclear strike on a U.S. city.

"The first indication [of such an attack] would be that the power would go out, and some, but not all, the telecommunications would go out. We would not physically feel anything in our bodies," Graham said.

As electric power, water and gas delivery systems failed, there would be "truly massive traffic jams," Graham added, since modern automobiles and signaling systems all depend on sophisticated electronics that would be disabled by the EMP wave.

"So you would be walking. You wouldn't be driving at that point," Graham said. "And it wouldn't do any good to call the maintenance or repair people because they wouldn't be able to get there, even if you could get through to them."

The food distribution system also would grind to a halt as cold-storage warehouses stockpiling perishables went offline. Even warehouses equipped with backup diesel generators would fail, because "we wouldn't be able to pump the fuel into the trucks and get the trucks to the warehouses," Graham said.

The United States "would quickly revert to an early 19th century type of country," except that we would have 10 times as many people with ten times fewer resources, he said.

"Most of the things we depend upon would be gone, and we would literally be depending on our own assets and those we could reach by walking to them," Graham said.

America would begin to resemble the 2002 TV series, "Jeremiah," which depicts a world bereft of law, infrastructure, and memory.

In the TV series, an unspecified virus wipes out the entire adult population of the planet. In an EMP attack, the casualties would be caused by our almost total dependence on technology for everything from food and water, to hospital care.

Within a week or two of the attack, people would start dying, Graham says.

"People in hospitals would be dying faster than that, because they depend on power to stay alive. But then it would go to water, food, civil authority, emergency services. And we would end up with a country with many, many people not surviving the event."

Asked just how many Americans would die if Iran were to launch the EMP attack it appears to be preparing, Graham gave a chilling reply.

"You have to go back into the 1800s to look at the size of population" that could survive in a nation deprived of mechanized agriculture, transportation, power, water, and communication.

"I'd have to say that 70 to 90 percent of the population would not be sustainable after this kind of attack," he said.

America would be reduced to a core of around 30 million people—about the number that existed in the decades after America's independence from Great Britain.

The modern electronic economy would shut down, and America would most likely revert to "an earlier economy based on barter," the EMP commission's report on Critical National Infrastructure concluded [in 2008].

> **FAST FACT**
>
> A poll conducted by the Israel Project found that 87 percent of Americans believe that a nuclear Iran would pose a threat to the United States.

In his recent congressional testimony, Graham revealed that Iranian military journals, translated by the CIA at his commission's request, "explicitly discuss a nuclear EMP attack that would gravely harm the United States."

Furthermore, if Iran launched its attack from a cargo ship plying the commercial sea lanes off the East coast—a scenario that appears to have been tested during the Caspian Sea tests—U.S. investigators might never determine who was behind the attack. Because of the limits of nuclear forensic technology, it could take months. And to disguise their traces, the Iranians could simply decide to sink the ship that had been used to launch it, Graham said.

Several participants in the conference in Dearborn, Mich., hosted by the conservative Claremont Institute argued that Iranian president Mahmoud Ahmadinejad was thinking about an EMP attack when he opined that "a world without America is conceivable."

In May 2007, then Undersecretary of State John Rood told Congress that the U.S. intelligence community estimates that Iran could develop an ICBM [intercontinental ballistic missile] capable of hitting the continental United States by 2015.

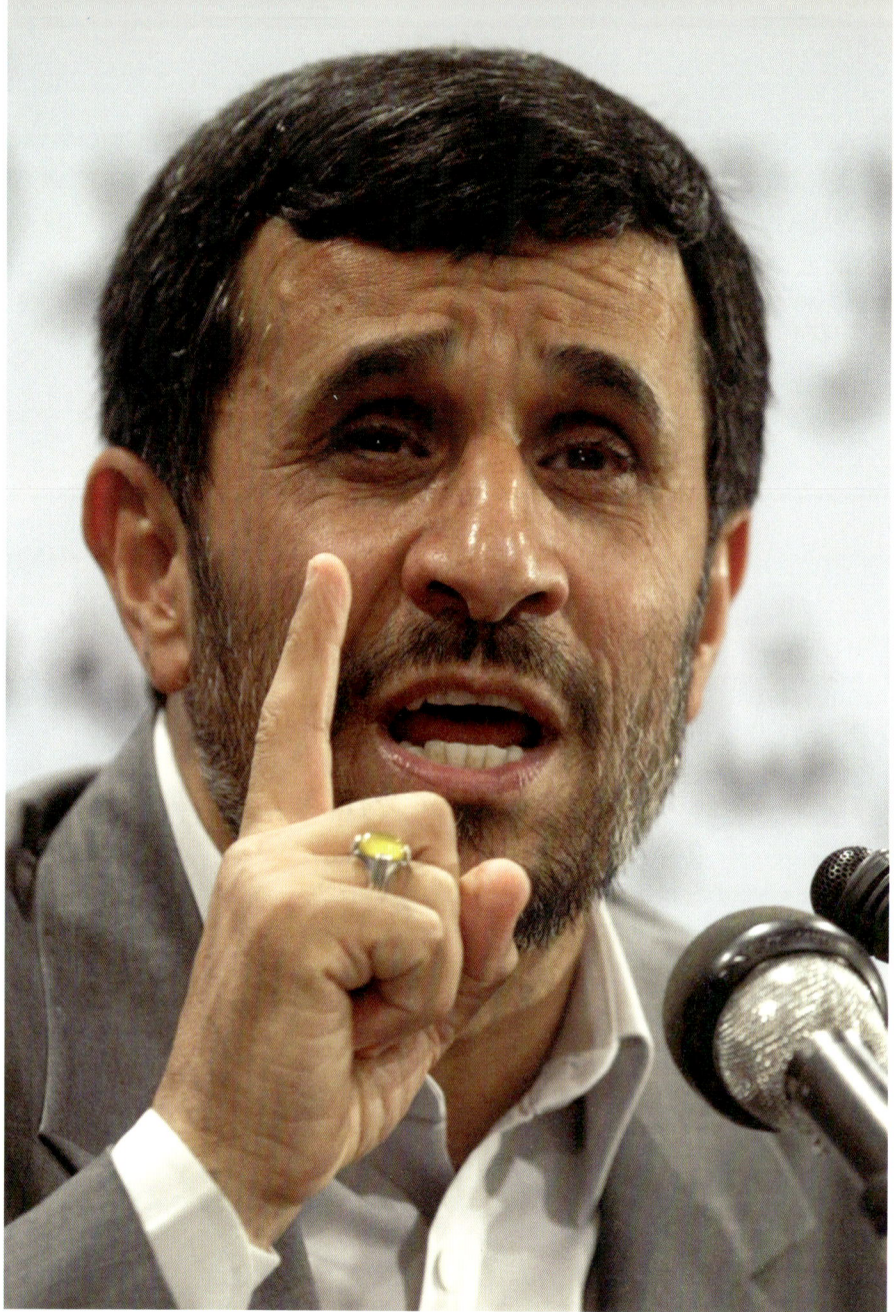

*Iranian president Mahmoud Ahmadinejad has threatened the United States and Israel with nuclear retaliation if they interfere with Iran's nuclear program.*

But Iran could put a Scud missile on board a cargo ship and launch from the commercial sea lanes off America's coasts well before then.

The only thing Iran is lacking for an effective EMP attack is a nuclear warhead, and no one knows with any certainty when that will occur. The latest U.S. intelligence estimate states that Iran could

16   Iran

acquire the fissile material for a nuclear weapon as early as 2009, or as late as 2015, or possibly later.

Secretary of Defense Donald Rumsfeld first detailed the "Scud-in-a-bucket" threat during a briefing in Huntsville, Ala., on Aug. 18, 2004.

While not explicitly naming Iran, Rumsfeld revealed that "one of the nations in the Middle East had launched a ballistic missile from a cargo vessel. They had taken a short-range, probably Scud missile, put it on a transporter-erector launcher, lowered it in, taken the vessel out into the water, peeled back the top, erected it, fired it, lowered it, and covered it up. And the ship that they used was using a radar and electronic equipment that was no different than 50, 60, 100 other ships operating in the immediate area."

Iran's first test of a ship-launched Scud missile occurred in spring 1998, and was mentioned several months later in veiled terms by the Commission to Assess the Ballistic Missile Threat to the United States, a blue-ribbon panel also known as the Rumsfeld Commission.

I was the first reporter to mention the Iran sea-launched missile test in an article appearing in the *Washington Times* in May 1999.

Intelligence reports on the launch were "well known to the White House but have not been disseminated to the appropriate congressional committees," I wrote. Such a missile "could be used in a devastating stealth attack against the United States or Israel for which the United States has no known or planned defense."

Few experts believe that Iran can be deterred from launching such an attack by the threat of massive retaliation against Iran. They point to a December 2001 statement by former Iranian President Ali Akbar Hashemi-Rafsanjani, who mulled the possibility of Israeli retaliation after an Iranian nuclear strike.

"The use of an atomic bomb against Israel would destroy Israel completely, while [the same] against the Islamic only would cause damages. Such a scenario is not inconceivable," Rafsanjani said at the time.

Rep. Trent Franks, R, Ariz., plans to introduce legislation that would require the Pentagon to lay the groundwork for an eventual military strike against Iran, to prevent Iran from acquiring nuclear weapons and EMP capability.

"An EMP attack on America would send us back to the horse and buggy era—without the horse and buggy," he told the Claremont Institute conference. "If you're a terrorist, this is your ultimate goal, your ultimate asymmetric weapon."

Noting Iran's recent sea-launched and mid-flight warhead detonation tests, Rep. Franks concluded, "They could do it—either directly or anonymously by putting some freighter out there on the ocean."

The only possible deterrent against Iran is the prospect of failure, Dr. Graham and other experts agreed. And the only way the United States could credibly threaten an Iranian missile strike would be to deploy effective national missile defenses.

"It's well known that people don't go on a diet until they've had a heart attack," said Claremont Institute president Brian T. Kennedy. "And we as a nation are having a heart attack" when it comes to the threat of an EMP attack from Iran.

"As of today, we have no defense against such an attack. We need space-based missile defenses to protect against an EMP attack," he told Newsmax.

Rep. Franks said he remains surprised at how partisan the subject of space-based missile defenses remain. "Nuclear missiles don't discriminate on party lines when they land," he said.

Arizona Republican Sen. Jon Kyl, a long-standing champion of missile defense, told the Claremont conference that [then] Sen. Obama has opposed missile defense tooth and nail and as president would cut funding for these programs dramatically.

"Senator Obama has been quoted as saying, 'I don't agree with a missile defense system,' and that we can cut $10 billion of the research out—never mind, as I say, that the entire budget is $9.6 billion, or $9.3 billion," Kyl said.

Like Franks, Kyl believes that the only way to eventually deter Iran from launching an EMP attack on the United States is to deploy robust missile defense systems, including space-based interceptors.

The United States "needs a missile defense that is so strong, in all the different phases we need to defend against . . . that countries will decide it's not worth coming up against us," Kyl said.

"That's one of the things that defeated the Soviet Union. That's one of the ways we can deal with these rogue states . . . and also the way that we can keep countries that are not enemies today, but are potential enemies, from developing capabilities to challenge us."

**EVALUATING THE AUTHORS' ARGUMENTS:**

In this viewpoint Timmerman argues that once Iran develops nuclear weapons it could use them to attack the United States. But not everyone agrees that Iran is developing nuclear weapons. Choose six authors in this book and write one sentence for each that explains 1) their position on whether Iran is developing nuclear weapons, and 2) whether Iran is a threat to the United States.

## Viewpoint 2

# Iran Does Not Pose a Serious Threat to the United States

### Phyllis Bennis

*"Even U.S. intelligence agencies agree that Iran doesn't possess nuclear weapons or a nuclear weapons program, and that it is very unclear whether Iran even wants to build such a weapon."*

In the following viewpoint Phyllis Bennis argues that Iran is not a threat to the United States. She explains that Iran does not yet have the military strength to compete with America, nor does it have nuclear weapons with which to threaten it. Bennis addresses the George W. Bush administration's claims that Iran is a threat to the United States point by point to reveal the unlikelihood of an attack on the United States by Iran. She argues that Iran does not represent a strategic military threat to the United States as it has a weak economy and has not invaded another country in over a century. For these reasons, Bennis says it is unlikely that Iran would attack the United States.

Bennis is a fellow of both the Institute for Policy Studies in Washington and the Transnational Institute in Amsterdam. A frequent commentator on *The NewsHour with Jim Lehrer* and the CBS *Morning Show*, she specializes in U.S. relations with the United Nations and Middle East politics.

Phyllis Bennis, "Understanding the U.S.-Iran Crisis," *Foreign Policy in Review*, October 13, 2008. Reproduced by permission.

**AS YOU READ, CONSIDER THE FOLLOWING QUESTIONS:**
1. How much did Iran spend on its military in 2007?
2. Does the Bush administration claim that Iran has a nuclear weapons program?
3. When did the U.S. ban on purchasing Iranian oil begin?

With George W. Bush's administration in its last year in office, the danger of a U.S. military attack on Iran still looms as a dangerous possibility. Widespread official government, military, and analytical sources, including the collective assessment of all sixteen U.S. intelligence agencies, have debunked the various pretexts being asserted to justify such an attack. But the continuing, ideologically driven extremism in the White House means that the danger of a reckless, unilateral military attack remains, and such an attack could happen despite the consequences.

This [viewpoint] is designed to address some of those fears, answer some of those questions, and propose some ideas to prevent those looming disaster.

*Is Iran a threat to the United States?*

The Bush administration has claimed, almost since coming into office, that Iran is a "threat" to the U.S. Even U.S. intelligence agencies agree that Iran doesn't possess nuclear weapons or a nuclear weapons program, and that it is very unclear whether Iran even wants to build such a weapon. Iran has never threatened the United States. (And unlike many countries in its neighborhood, Iran has not invaded another country in over a century.)

In 2007, according to the CIA, Iran spent about $5.1 billion on its military—about 2.5 percent of its GDP [gross domestic product]. The U.S., on the other hand, spent $626 billion on the military that same year, amounting to 4.5 percent of its GDP of $13.7 trillion. More relevant, perhaps, the U.S. spent almost half of the total of global arms spending—about 46 percent. So Iran does not represent a strategic military threat to the United States or to Americans.

[Iranian president Mahmoud] Ahmadinejad's political opposition to Israel has never been in doubt, but still his statements were distorted. Outrage erupted across the U.S. and Europe in October 2005 following the claim that Ahmadinejad had threatened to "wipe Israel off the map." . . . But as it turned out, Ahmadinejad had not said those words at all. "Ahmadinejad did not say he was going to wipe Israel off the map because no such idiom exists," Juan Cole, a Middle East expert at the University of Michigan told the *New York Times*. "He did say he hoped its regime, i.e., a Jewish-Zionist state occupying Jerusalem, would collapse." Cole went on to note that since Iran has not "attacked another country aggressively for over a century, I smell the whiff of war propaganda."

[In April 2006] Bush repeated . . . "we've agreed on the goal, and that is the Iranians should not have a nuclear weapon, the capacity to make a nuclear weapon, or the knowledge as to how to make a nuclear weapon." The significance of that language lay in the uncontested reality that Iran already had, indeed has had for many years, "the knowledge as to how to make a nuclear weapon." Not only because much of that knowledge is available on the internet, but because the basic technology needed to enrich uranium for nuclear power is the same as that required for nuclear weapons. Of course it is easier to carry out the 3–5 percent enrichment needed for nuclear power than the 90-plus percent enrichment necessary to produce weapons-grade uranium. But the technology is the same. Once you have the knowledge to build and run the centrifuges to enrich uranium, you just need time and money and practice to enrich enough for a bomb. You also do need missile technology, but like many countries around the world, Iran already had that, too. Bush's bar for bombing Iran could hardly get any lower.

*Does Iran have nuclear weapons or a nuclear weapons program?*

No. Iran does not and has never had a nuclear weapon—and no one, not even the Bush administration, claims it has. Despite claims by the Bush administration and others, there is also no evidence Iran has a military program to build nuclear weapons. And even the Bush administration's own intelligence agencies acknowledged in

**FAST FACT**

A national intelligence estimate released in 2007 reports that Iran halted its nuclear weapons program in 2003.

the December 2007 National Intelligence Estimate that the weapons program they claim once existed had been ended by 2003.

*What about Iran's support for terrorism?*

Since the 1979 overthrow of the U.S.-backed shah of Iran, the accusation of Iran being a "state supporter of terrorism" has been a hallmark of U.S. policy. The State Department's 2007 *Country Reports on Terrorism* . . . states that "Iran remains a threat to regional stability and U.S. interests in the Middle East because of its continued support for violent groups, such as HAMAS and Hizballah, and its efforts to undercut the democratic process in Lebanon, where it seeks to build Iran's and Hizballah's influence to the detriment of other Lebanese communities." There is no evidence and little detail provided, beyond the broad claim that Iran is providing "extensive funding, training, and weapons" to those groups. The report does not acknowledge that both the most important "Palestinian group with leadership in Syria," Hamas, and Hezbollah in Lebanon are important political parties that have been democratically elected to majority and near-majority positions in their respective parliaments. Both, while certainly maintaining military wings, also provide important networks of social services, from clinics and hospitals to schools, daycare centers, food assistance and financial aid to the impoverished, disempowered, and (in the case of Hamas in Gaza) imprisoned populations of Lebanese and Palestinians. Some of the actions carried out by the military wings of Hamas and Hezbollah have in fact targeted civilians in violation of international law, and thus might qualify as "terrorist" actions. But the majority of their actions have been aimed at illegal Israeli military occupations: of south Lebanon in the case of Hezbollah, and of Gaza and the West Bank in the case of Hamas. The notion that Iran's support for these elected organizations, if it exists, somehow puts Iran at the top of the list of states supporting terrorism, let alone gives the US the right to attack, has no legitimacy.

The State Department report goes on to condemn Iran for remaining "unwilling to bring to justice senior al-Qaeda (AQ) members it has detained, and has refused to publicly identify those senior members in its custody. Iran has repeatedly resisted numerous calls to transfer custody of its AQ detainees to their countries of origin or third countries for interrogation or trial." Given more than six years of the Bush administration's own "unwillingness to bring to justice senior al-Qaeda members it detained in 2003" and even earlier in Guantánamo, and the U.S.'s "refusal to identify publicly these senior members in its custody" and its continued resistance to "numerous calls to transfer custody of its al-Qaeda detainees to their countries of origin or to third countries for interrogation and/or trial" the hypocrisy of claiming this as evidence of support for terrorism is astonishing.

*What false claims has the Bush administration made about Iran?*

On the nuclear weapons issue, it is false to claim that Iran is violating the Non-Proliferation Treaty (NPT) by enriching uranium for its nuclear power plants. The NPT (Article IV) allows every country that signs on as a non–nuclear weapons state, including Iran, the inalienable right "to develop research, production and use of nuclear energy for peaceful purposes without discrimination." Further, the treaty actually encourages its signatories to spread the development of nuclear power, and states explicitly that all its signatories "have the right to participate in the fullest possible exchange of equipment, materials and *scientific and technological* information for the peaceful uses of nuclear energy" (emphasis added). So much for Iran breaking the law through knowledge. The NPT's enforcement agency, the International Atomic Energy Agency [IAEA], has consistently reported that it has no evidence of Iran diverting nuclear materials or programs to military purposes. While the IAEA [the UN's nuclear watchdog agency] has been concerned about insufficient transparency in some of Iran's reports, that does not constitute a violation of the NPT. (Iran has rejected the Security Council's demand that it halt all nuclear enrichment activities; those resolutions themselves stand in contradiction to the guaranteed right to produce nuclear power that is central to the Non-Proliferation Treaty.)

It is false to claim that Iran is responsible for the deaths of U.S. troops in Iraq. There is no question that Iranians—businesspeople, diplomats, aid workers, others—are operating in Iraq; they share a long border and a longer history. But there has been no direct evidence—only assertions—presented to back up the claim that the Iranian government has provided Iraqi militias with "explosively formed penetrators" (EFPs) or any other weapons.

Another set of false claims concern President Ahmadinejad. Certainly much of his rhetoric, clearly designed to bolster his populist domestic base, has been inflammatory and offensive—particularly his questioning of the reality of the Nazi Holocaust. (He has also become well known for his remark at Columbia University denying that there are homosexuals in Iran—although this appeared to be a one-off reference, not part of his ordinary discourse, it is still horrifyingly homophobic, as well as preposterous.) But instead of criticizing the real outrages, U.S. political and media figures have made exaggerated and false claims to rebut and created straw men to knock down.

*Some experts say that because Iran's economy is so dependent on selling oil to Western countries, it cannot afford to upset Western customers by going nuclear.*

How Dangerous Is the Threat from Iran?   25

*What could Iran do in response to a U.S. military strike?*

A wide range of possibilities would be open to Iran. While U.S. officials might call a military attack "only a surgical strike," Iran would certainly call it an act of war—which would indeed be an accurate term. Iran could send troops across its borders to attack U.S. troops in Iraq or shoot missiles into occupied Baghdad's U.S.-controlled Green Zone. Iranian troops could invade and occupy southern Iraq. Iran could attack U.S. troop concentrations in Kuwait, Oman, Qatar, or elsewhere in the region, or go after U.S. ships in Bahrain, home of the Navy's Fifth Fleet. It could attack Israel. It could retaliate against U.S. or allied oil tankers in nearby shipping lanes, and even sink a tanker. It could close the Strait of Hormuz, through which 45 percent of the world's oil passes. The impact on the world economic system would be swift and devastating.

In conventional terms, Iran's military is no match for the U.S. Iran has faced years of military sanctions, and its military strategy is focused primarily on training troops to defend the homeland against invasion and foreign military occupation.

*Where does oil fit into the U.S. policy towards Iran?*

Oil has always been central to U.S. relations with Iran, despite the U.S. ban on purchasing Iranian oil since 1979. For a global power such as the U.S., the issue is not so much direct access to Iran's oil—the U.S. doesn't need to import that much Iranian or indeed Middle Eastern oil in general for its own use. Far more important is maintaining control of Iran's and other countries' oil supplies: the ability to determine price and to guarantee access to oil to favored friends and deny it to competitors.

The crusade to gain control of strategic resources, especially oil, remains a hallmark of the so-called global war on terror, the Bush administration's banner covering its wars in Afghanistan and Iraq, attacks on Somalia and expansion of military bases across the Middle East.

*Do U.S. sanctions against Iran work? What are the costs?*

Sanctions and isolation of Iran were Washington's strategy throughout the 1990s. Although the U.S. sanctions against Iran were not nearly as extreme as those the U.S. imposed on Iraq in the name of the United Nations, the Iranian people still have paid a steep price. Much of Iran's infrastructure—particularly its oil infrastructure and

# Iran Does Not Pose a Military Threat to the United States

A side-by-side comparison of the military capability of the United States and Iran shows that the Iranian military is no match for the United States.

| | United States | Iran |
|---|---|---|
| Population | 303,824,646 | 65,875,223 |
| Gross domestic product (GDP) | $13.8 trillion | $0.75 trillion |
| Defense spending fiscal year 2009 | $711 billion | $7.2 billion |
| Total troops | 2,580,875 | 895,000 |
| Main battle tanks | 8,023 | 1,613 |
| Reconnaissance vehicles | 348 | 35 |
| Armored infantry fighting vehicles | 6,719 | 610 |
| Armored personnel carriers | 21,242 | 640 |
| Artillery units | 8,041 | 8,196 |
| Helicopters | 5,425 | 311 |
| Submarines | 71 | 6 |
| Principal surface combatants | 106 | 5 |
| Patrol and coastal combatants | 157 | 320 |
| Mine warfare ships | 9 | 5 |
| Amphibious ships | 490 | 21 |
| Fighter aircraft | 3,538 | 286 |
| Long-range bomber aircraft | 170 | None |
| Transport aircraft | 883 | 136 |
| Electronic warfare/intelligence aircraft | 159 | 3 |
| Reconnaissance aircraft | 134 | 6 |
| Maritime patrol aircraft | 197 | 8 |
| Anti-submarine warfare aircraft | 58 | None |
| Airborne early warning aircraft | 53 | None |
| Nuclear warheads | 5,400 | None |

Taken from: Center for Arms Control and Non-proliferation, July 7, 2008.

civilian airlines—was created during the shah's regime, so most spare parts required are of U.S. make and thus unavailable under the sanctions. In June 2005, a report prepared for the International Civil Air Aviation Organization "warned that U.S. sanctions against Iran were placing civilian lives in danger by denying Iranian aviation necessary spare parts and aircraft repair. . . ." Six months later, a U.S.-made military transport plane crashed, killing 108 people.

When imposed by the biggest economy in the world, "unilateral" sanctions invariably take a multilateral toll, since other countries and financial institutions are eager to stay on Washington's good side. Even so-called smart sanctions, designed only to target those tied directly to Iran's nuclear industry, end up affecting large numbers of people. Designating Iran's entire Revolutionary Guard Corps as a "terrorist entity," as the Bush administration did in late 2007, imposes sanctions on tens or perhaps hundreds of thousands of Iranians whose family members have ties to that huge bureaucracy within Iran's official military.

Oil sanctions diminish Iran's ability to rebuild and improve its seriously eroded oil-refining capacity, thus reducing the amount of gasoline and other oil-based products available for domestic use. And, ironically, the sanctions themselves cause more Iranians to believe that their country needs nuclear power, despite its massive oil reserves, because of the sanctions-driven shortages of refined oil-based fuels.

*What could—and should—U.S. relations with Iran look like?*

Any serious effort to minimize tensions and normalize relations between the United States and Iran must recognize that negotiations and diplomacy, not sanctions, military threats, or military attacks, must be the basis of the U.S. posture toward Iran. The United States should also recognize that the United Nations, through the International Atomic Energy Agency (not the Security Council), should be the central actor in orchestrating international negotiations with Iran. The United States should agree to be bound by international legal prohibitions as well as the global consensus against any military strike against Iran.

Any negotiations between the United States and Iran must recognize what Iran actually wants: a security guarantee (guaranteeing no invasion, no attack on nuclear facilities, and no efforts at "regime change"), recognition of Iran's role as an indigenous regional power, and reaffirmation of Iran's rights under the Non-Proliferation Treaty. Once those rights are internationally affirmed, it will be up to Iran itself to determine whether and with whom they will negotiate on how those rights are to be implemented.

The consequences of the United States having severed all diplomatic ties with Iran since 1979 should be recognized and Washington should move urgently to reestablish full diplomatic relations with Tehran.

*What can we, the people, do to prevent a U.S. war on Iran?*

We must increase the political cost for any politician or policymaker even considering or threatening the use of a military strike against Iran.

Active mobilization against an attack on Iran is crucial. Certainly such mobilization will be challenging, but we must confront and overcome the skepticism about the value of antiwar protest that has been created by years of Washington's rejection of the demands of the even larger and longer-standing movement opposing the Iraq war.

The strong majority agreement across the United States, and the near unanimity in the rest of the world, that the Iraq war has been a disaster for Iraq, for the U.S., for the region and for the world, means that there is even less support for launching another, equally or even more disastrous war in Iran. There is still time. We have a powerful movement experienced in mobilizing and we have seven years of success in changing public opinion. We can do it again. We must.

### EVALUATING THE AUTHOR'S ARGUMENTS:

Phyllis Bennis quotes from several sources to support the points she makes in her article. Make a list of everyone she quotes, including their credentials and the nature of their comments. Then, analyze her sources—are they credible? Are they well qualified to speak on this subject? Choose one quote that particularly grabbed you and helped convince you of the author's argument.

# Viewpoint 3

# Iran Poses a Serious Threat to Israel

## HonestReporting

Iran seeks the destruction of Israel, HonestReporting argues in the following viewpoint. The author reports that Iranian president Mahmoud Ahmadinejad has clearly stated his desire to see Israel wiped off the map of nations. Ahmadinejad blames Israel for the lack of peace in the Middle East and resents that Western nations have so heavily supported it. The author warns that Iran has developed long-range missiles that could easily launch a nuclear warhead from Iran toward one of Israel's major cities. Such an attack would destroy buildings and infrastructure and kill countless people. To protect itself from the Iranian threat, the author says that Israel must either diplomatically deal with Iran or use its military to prevent an impending crisis.

HonestReporting is an independent nonprofit organization dedicated to defending Israel against media prejudice. Formed in 2000 by a group of British students, HonestReporting monitors the media, exposes cases of bias, and provides educational tools and resources to anyone wishing to advocate for Israel.

*"Iranian President Mahmoud Ahmadinejad has stated that Israel should not exist."*

HonestReporting, "Iran: A Threat to Israel and the World," January 15, 2007. Reproduced by permission.

## AS YOU READ, CONSIDER THE FOLLOWING QUESTIONS:
1. According to the author, in what year did Iranian president Mahmoud Ahmadinejad call for Israel to be "wiped off the face of the map?"
2. What type of Iranian missile does the author say could be launched toward the Israeli city of Tel Aviv?
3. A nuclear attack by Iran toward the Israeli city of Tel Aviv could kill how many people who live in the metropolitan area, according to the author?

Although most of the world press has done an admirable job reporting on the developments of the Iranian nuclear program, the threat to both Israel and the world that Iran presents cannot be understated. . . . It is currently unclear what actions, diplomatic or military, will eventually be used to stop the Iranian nuclear program. Nonetheless, everyone should be aware of the threat and Iran's pursuit of nuclear weapons capability.

## Iranian Policy Says Israel Should Not Exist

Time and time again, Iranian President Mahmoud Ahmadinejad has stated that Israel should not exist. Moreover, he has done so with no significant domestic dissent. When the leader of a sovereign nation makes unequivocal statements without domestic opposition, those statements serve as the basis of national policy. It is critical to note that Ahmadinejad's statements go beyond opposition to Israeli policies, he is speaking of Israel's very existence.

In 2005, much of the media reported his call for Israel (actually the "Zionist regime" since Iran refuses to use the word "Israel") to be "wiped off the face of the map" in a keynote address to the Iranian-government sponsored "World without Zionism" conference. Such sponsorship is, in itself, incitement to genocide. Neither the United States, Israel, or any other nation has ever sponsored a conference themed on the destruction of another country.

There are those who say that Ahmadinejad was misquoted. Yet in a June 11, 2006 analysis, *New York Times* deputy foreign editor Ethan Bronner concluded that:

translators in Tehran who work for the president's office and the (Iranian) foreign ministry disagree with (those who say he was misquoted). All official translations of Mr. Ahmadinejad's statement refer to wiping Israel away.

At other times, Ahmadinejad has said:
- "The real cure for the conflict is elimination of the Zionist regime."
- "The way to peace in the Middle East is the destruction of Israel."
- "Like it or not, the Zionist regime is heading toward annihilation."
- "The Zionist regime is a rotten, dried tree that will be eliminated by one storm."

## "Incitement to Commit Genocide"

In addition, almost all senior leaders of Iran have made similar statements. What is especially alarming is that these statements are not aimed at Israeli policies, but rather at the nation of Israel as a whole. As the Jerusalem Center for Public Affairs has pointed out in its "Referral of Iranian President Ahmadinejad on the Charge of Incitement to Commit Genocide"...

> It is essential to distinguish between freedom to oppose a government and incitement to genocide. Verbal barrages (against a government) pose no existential threat to ordinary people in the street. Ahmadinejad's reckless anti-Semitic tirades that "the Jews are very filthy people," "[the Jews have] inflicted the most damage on the human race," "[the Jews are] a bunch of bloodthirsty barbarians," "they should know that they are nearing the last days of their lives," and "as the Imam said, Israel must be wiped off the map" should have aroused trepidation. His apocalyptic utterances are not mere rhetoric. Ahmadinejad's declaration that the Holocaust was a "fairy tale," and his enabling of Hamas and Hizbullah [Palestinian and Lebanese political organizations], demonstrate that there is simply no way for his ambitions to be realized without perpetrating a new genocide.

Speaking to students in Tehran, Iranian president Mahmoud Ahmadinejad denies that the Holocaust occurred and threatens Israel with destruction.

## Iran Is Developing Long Range Missiles

Years before the current controversy involving Iran's attempts to develop nuclear power and (according to almost all experts) nuclear weapons, Iran invested heavily in the acquisition of long range missile systems. When coupled with nuclear warheads, these missiles would give Iran the ability to threaten countries far from its borders. According to Uzi Rubin, a prominent military analyst:

> The Iranians are pursuing the most intensive missile program in the Third World, with constantly increasing ranges.

How Dangerous Is the Threat from Iran? 33

The Iranian Shahab 3 missile (domestically produced within Iran) can threaten either [Israeli city] Tel Aviv or [Saudi Arabian city] Riyadh from the same launch point. The newer Shahab 3ER, with its 2,000 km range, can reach Ankara in Turkey, Alexandria in Egypt, or Sanaa in Yemen from one single launch point deep within Iran. Thus, Iran does not have to move its launchers to project power, making its missile arsenal more survivable.

Yet even this missile does not appear to be enough for Iran. According to the *Washington Times*:

> In January (2006), the German magazine *Bild* reported that Iran purchased 18 BM-25 land-mobile missiles from North Korea. The BM-25 is a variation of the SS-N-6, a Soviet–made submarine-launched ballistic missile, with a range of up to 1,800 miles. The BM-25, according to Mr. Rubin, "is a nuclear missile.... There is no other warhead for this other than a nuclear warhead." The Iranian missile threat is clearly growing.

Finally, Iran's ultimate goal seems to be the ability to strike anywhere, including the United States. The Center for Strategic and International Studies took a look at Iranian research plans. They noted that:

> ... Iran is attempting to create a Shahab-5 and a Shahab-6, with a 3,000–5,000 kilometer range. These missiles would be three-stage rockets. If completed, the Shahab-5 and the Shahab-6 would take Iran into the realm of limited range ICBM's [intercontinental ballistic missles], and enable Iran to target the US eastern seaboard.

### Iran's Nuclear Program Is Not for Peaceful Purposes

Iran's efforts are clearly aimed at the production of nuclear weapons. Iran's declarations that its nuclear program is for peaceful purposes lacks any credibility. In August of 2004, former U.S. Representative to the United Nations John Bolton testified that:

> Cover stories put forward by Iran for the development of a nuclear fuel cycle and for individual facilities are simply not

credible. For example, Iran is making an enormous investment in facilities to mine, process, and enrich uranium, and says it needs to make its own reactor fuel because it cannot count on foreign supplies. But for at least the next decade Iran will have at most a single nuclear power reactor. In addition, Iran does not have enough indigenous uranium resources to fuel even one power-generating reactor over its lifetime—though it has quite enough uranium to make several nuclear bombs. We are being asked to believe that Iran is building uranium enrichment capacity to make fuel for reactors that do not exist from uranium Iran does not have.

> **FAST FACT**
>
> In March 2009 Revolutionary Guard commander Mohammad Ali Jafari reported that Iran has missiles with a range of 2,000 km (1,250 miles)—capable of reaching targets within Israel.

### Israel Would Not Survive a Nuclear Attack

While even the "smallest" nuclear attack anywhere is an unimaginable horror, because of its size and population, it would be almost impossible for the country of Israel to survive a single nuclear attack.

The following is an account of the atomic bomb dropped on Hiroshima, considered primitive and tiny compared to modern nuclear weapons.

> The bomb exploded about 600 meters (2,000 ft) above the city with a blast equivalent to about 13 kilotons of TNT (the U-235 weapon was considered very inefficient, with only 1.38% of its material fissioning), instantly killing at least an estimated 90,000 people. The radius of total destruction was about 1.6 km (1 mile), with resulting fires across 11.4 square km (4.4 square miles). Infrastructure damage was estimated at 90% of Hiroshima's buildings being either damaged or completely destroyed.
>
> Such an attack, again using one of the smallest and least effective nuclear weapons . . . could result in the deaths of most of the 1,190,000 people who live within the Tel Aviv metropolitan district.

Furthermore, radioactive fall-out would spread rapidly not only to all parts of Israel, but across the Middle East and even to Europe with certain wind conditions. The world's economies would be devastated and millions of people would become instant refugees.

## Iran Must Be Stopped

The destruction of Israel is a stated goal of the government of Iran. In light of Iran's relentless drive to acquire nuclear weapons, it is clear that action must be taken to avert the threat. Since ensuring survival is the prime obligation of a sovereign state towards its own citizens, diplomatic or other actions against Iran should be considered legitimate acts of self-defense and supported by the world community.

Taken from: Charles Gauske, "The War of Words over Missile Defense," Russiablog.org, June 18, 2007.

## EVALUATING THE AUTHOR'S ARGUMENTS:

HonestReporting describes how the Iranian president's ambitions to destroy Israel threaten the nation. What do you think? Do you think Iran poses a serious threat to Israel, or do you think Ahmadinejad is all talk? Do you think Iran is actually able to launch such an attack? Explain your position using evidence from the texts you have read.

# Viewpoint 4

# Iran Does Not Pose a Serious Threat to Israel

## Leon Hadar

*"Even if Iran acquired nuclear weapons, it would not pose an 'existential' threat to Israel."*

In the following viewpoint Leon Hadar argues that Iran does not pose a serious threat to Israel. While the two countries have an unfriendly relationship, and although Iran has threatened to destroy Israel in the past, Hadar does not think Iran has the nuclear weapons with which to attack Israel. Even if Iran were to acquire nuclear weapons, he says, it would probably not attack Israel out of fear of an Israeli counterattack. Indeed, Israel is believed to have hundreds of nuclear weapons in its arsenal and could obliterate Iran. Furthermore, it is likely that Western nations such as the United States would come to Israel's defense. As such, Israel is able to deter any potential threat of attack from Iran. Furthermore, Hadar explains that Israel would like to resolve the conflict between the two countries diplomatically—if Iran were willing, Israel would probably engage in talks to defuse the nuclear crisis. He concludes that until Iran develops nuclear weapons on a par with Israel's supply, it does not pose a threat to Israel.

Leon Hadar, "Look Who's Downplaying Iran's Nuclear Threat," AntiWar.com, November 22, 2007. Reproduced by permission of the author.

Hadar is a research fellow in foreign policy studies. He is the former United Nations bureau chief for *The Jerusalem Post* and is currently the Washington correspondent for *The Singapore Business Times.* He is also the author of *Sandstorm: Policy Failure in the Middle East* and *Quagmire: America in the Middle East.*

**AS YOU READ, CONSIDER THE FOLLOWING QUESTIONS:**
1. How would Israel deal with Iran if Iran does acquire nuclear weapons, according to the author?
2. As reported by Hadar, how many nuclear weapons does Israel have?
3. In what year does Hadar say Iran was willing to negotiate with both the United States and Israel about a regional settlement?

Imagine Secretary of State Condoleezza Rice telling a group of leading U.S. policymakers that Iran's nuclear weapons program does not pose a direct threat to U.S. security, or former CIA Director George Tenet making the same kind of argument in a public forum. Imagine also that their views are reported in front-page news stories in the *Washington Post* and the *New York Times.*

You don't have to be a veteran Washington insider to predict that in the aftermath of a *Times* headline like "Rice: U.S. Can Live with Iran Bomb," America's chief diplomat would be forced to resign, but her comments would dramatically transform the debate in Washington. At a minimum, President George W. Bush might stop threatening [Iranian capital] Tehran with a military response if it decides to go nuclear. Instead, most of the discussion in the U.S. capital would focus on the "Day After"—that is, on ways to deter Iran from using its nuclear military capability.

## U.S. Officials Hype the Threat from Iran

But if that happens, and U.S. officials agree with MIT's Barry Posen and other American strategists that Iranian nukes would *not* pose a direct threat to America, wouldn't Norman Podhoretz and other neoconservatives then argue that nuclear arms in the hands of Iranian President Mahmoud Ahmadinejad could endanger the security of

Israel and create a condition for another Holocaust? And in that case, shouldn't America "do something" to protect the interests of its ally, Israel?

Actually, neoconservatives are already making this kind of argument. Podhoretz, who is serving as a foreign policy adviser to Republican presidential candidate Rudy Giuliani, said that Ahmadinejad is "like Hitler" who wants to replace the international system with "the religio-political culture of Islamofascism." And Sen. Jon Kyl (R-AZ), invoking the same Ahmadinejad-is-Hitler analogy, recalled that, "During the run up to World War II, Europe failed to heed the warnings" about the threat that Nazi Germany posed to the world.

## Iran Cannot Destroy Israel

But Podhoretz and company could have difficulties presenting a case for going to war against Iran in order to protect Israel—both Israel's foreign minister and a former head of the Mossad, Israel's intelligence agency, have suggested that if Iran does acquire

"Inside Iran's Secret Rocket Building Site," cartoon by Nik Scott, Australia, April 12, 2008, PoliticalCartoons.com. Copyright © 2008 Nik Scott, Australia, and PoliticalCartoons.com. All rights reserved.

40   Iran

nuclear weapons, Israel would deal with it by *deterring* Iran. Not attacking it.

Indeed, according to a report published in Israel's *Ha'aretz* newspaper, Israeli Foreign Minister Tzipi Livni said in a series of closed discussions with other top Israeli officials that in her opinion Iranian nuclear weapons "do not pose an existential threat to Israel." In their report, which received very little attention in the United States, Gidi Weitz and Na'ama Lanski noted that "Livni also criticized the exaggerated use that Prime Minister Ehud Olmert is making of the issue of the Iranian bomb," claiming that he was "attempting to rally the public around him by playing on its most basic fears." Mmm . . . sound familiar?

*Ha'aretz* also reported in October [2007] that former Mossad Chief Efraim Halevy told an audience that even if Iran acquired nuclear weapons, it would not pose an

> **FAST FACT**
>
> According to the Nuclear Threat Initiative (NTI), Israel was the sixth nation in the world to develop nuclear weapons—and the first in the Middle East.

"existential" threat to Israel. During a lecture [in October 2007] in Jerusalem, Halevy—who, like Livni, is regarded as a "hawk"[1] on Israeli security—said that "the State of Israel cannot be destroyed" if Iran went nuclear. He also called on the government to follow Washington's lead and offer Iran a diplomatic option as part of a strategy to foil Tehran's nuclear plan.

"Israel cannot be destroyed for many reasons, some of which are known and others you can presume," Halevy said. "There is a chance that something serious will happen here, but I tend to say the following when I am abroad: Israel cannot be destroyed. If you do not believe this, then don't, but I suggest that you do not try it."

## Israel's Military Capabilities Would Deter Iran

Halevy seemed to be implying that Israel's own nuclear military capability (Israel is estimated to have about 300 nuclear weapons)

---

1. An advocate of aggressive political policies.

*The author says that the Israeli defense force, with its advanced resources on land, air, and sea, could effectively deter any threat from Iran.*

would be effective in deterring a nuclear Iran from attacking Israel. The former Mossad chief also downplayed the notion that has been promoted by neoconservatives that Iran is emerging as a regional and global threat, insisting that contrary to such rhetoric, the Iranians "are no giants." (The United States spends around 100 times as much as Iran does on its military).

## Israel More Likely than the United States to Negotiate with Iran

And Halevy called on Israel and the United States to negotiate with Iran a diplomatic deal along the lines proposed by the Iraq Study Group. (According to the *Financial Times* and other news reports,

Iran indicated its willingness in 2003 to negotiate with the United States a regional settlement that would have included recognition of Israel, but the Bush administration dismissed the proposal.)

It was not surprising therefore that the *Ha'aretz* correspondent who reported Halevy's comments added: "Halevy's lecture presented a less-disturbing picture from the one offered by President George W. Bush."

Indeed, notwithstanding the fact that Bush and Vice President Dick Cheney continue to insist publicly that they would like to resolve the nuclear crisis with Iran through diplomatic means, the two together with their aides and legions of supporters on Capitol Hill seem to be preparing for World War III. In an October 21 [2007] speech at the Washington Institute for Near East Policy, Cheney declared that the Bush administration will not stand by in the face of "the Iranian regime's efforts to destabilize the Middle East and to gain hegemonic power"; just a few days earlier, President Bush warned that if "you're interested in avoiding World War III, it seems like you ought to be interested in preventing [Iran] from having the knowledge necessary to make a nuclear weapon."

That Israeli hawks Livni and Halevy seem to be projecting a more realpolitik [practical political] approach toward Iran than Bush and Cheney, not to mention Republican frontrunner Giuliani's Podhoretz-led team of foreign policy advisers, is not unexpected.

## The United States Should Not Attack Iran to Protect Israel

There is no doubt that many Israelis had hoped that the United States would attack and perhaps destroy Iran's nuclear military installations—not because they are concerned about its threat to the existence of Israel, but because they are aware that a nuclear Iran would be able to challenge Israel's military supremacy in the Middle East. But there is now a growing recognition among Israeli officials that the Americans don't have the capability to decimate Iran's nuclear military sites and that a U.S. strike against Iran would, in all probability, lead to a U.S.-Iran military confrontation that could ignite a bloody regional war involving Hezbollah [Lebanese political and military organization] and Syria.

At the end of the day, the costs of such a war to Israelis would be higher than for the Americans, who could always go back home to the United States, where Podhoretz and his chicken-hawks would continue pushing for war from the safety of their offices.

> **EVALUATING THE AUTHOR'S ARGUMENTS:**
>
> Leon Hadar quotes from several sources to support the points he makes in his essay. Make a list of all the people he quotes, including their credentials and the nature of their comments. Then, analyze his sources: Are they credible? Are they well qualified to speak on the subject?

## Viewpoint 5

# Iran Poses a Threat to the Fragile Nation of Iraq

## Jeffrey White

*"Iran's leaders are ruthless, clever, and willing to take risks in Iraq."*

In the following viewpoint Jeffrey White argues that Iran threatens the fragile nation of Iraq. As neighbors in the Middle East, Iran and Iraq have a long and tenuous relationship. Currently, Iran seeks to gain influence and control in the war-struck nation of Iraq, White explains. Iraq is vulnerable to such an effort, as the multiyear war there by U.S. forces and their allies have severely weakened the country. Iran has infiltrated Iraq's social systems, political parties, and even religious circles. In fact, White says, Iran has even provided financial assistance to Iraqi extremist organizations. By embedding its people deeply into the fabric of Iraq, White warns, Iran will achieve a greater foothold in the Middle East. He concludes that Iran will likely continue to pretend to be a friend to Iraq so that it has greater access and resources to use against the United States and its other enemies.

Jeffrey White, "Fighting Iran in Iraq," Washington Institute of Near East Policy, February 14, 2007. Reproduced by permission.

White is a defense fellow at the Washington Institute. He specializes in Iraq military and security concerns. He is also a former Middle East intelligence analyst who worked for the U.S. Defense Intelligence Agency.

**AS YOU READ, CONSIDER THE FOLLOWING QUESTIONS:**
1. According to White, what Iranian weapons have U.S. officials discovered in Iraq?
2. What five tools does the author say Iran has for wielding influence in Iraq?
3. What three primary areas does Iran use to smuggle arms across the Iran-Iraq border, according to White?

The February 11 [2007] intelligence briefing in Baghdad [Iraq] revealed specific information about the transfer of weapons and weapons technology to Iranian allies in Iraq. This has furthered an extensive discussion of Iran's role in Iraq, especially as it relates to violence in the region. The involvement of Iran's clerical [religious] regime in Iraq is not new, or simple. It can be measured in decades, and is multifaceted and comprehensive, demanding an equally broad response from the United States and U.S. allies.

Iran's preferred outcome is that Iraq be dominated by Shiite elements under the sway—if not the direct control—of the Iranian regime. Iran may not be interested in having a collapsed state next door, but it has no interest in a viable Iraqi government independent of [Iranian capital] Tehran, standing as a symbol of American success in the region. If it cannot dominate the nation, a weak and conflict-ridden Iraq will at least serve Iran's interests. More broadly, in the wider contest between Tehran and Washington, Iran is exploiting U.S. involvement in Iraq to weaken U.S. capabilities and will.

## Iranian Weapons Found in Iraq

The Iranian challenge in Iraq has at least six major dimensions:

*Military.* The United States has now provided concrete evidence of Iranian weapons in Iraq, including rocket-propelled grenades, 81mm and 60mm mortar rounds, and components for improvised explosive devices (IEDs) with explosively formed penetrators. The latter are especially important because they are capable of penetrating the armor on the heaviest coalition vehicles. At least 170 American soldiers have been killed by these devices. Press reports also indicate that over 100 fifty-caliber sniper rifles, sold to Iran by Austria, were found during a raid on an arms cache in Baghdad. Even at long range, these weapons are capable of penetrating the body armor worn by coalition troops, as well as many lightly armored vehicles.

Iran also provides military training and advice to its allies and accomplices in Iraq. These activities are carried out by the elite Quds (Jerusalem) Force, a component of the Islamic Revolutionary Guard Corps (IRGC), and one of the principal groups that Iran uses to conduct clandestine operations. Quds Force leaders are close to the most senior leadership of the regime, including Supreme Leader Ali Hussein Khamenei. The IRGC commander himself has stated that

*In February 2007 the U.S. Army displayed Iranian weapons found in Iraq as proof that Iran is interfering in Iraq's affairs.*

## Iran's Presence in Iraq

Located next to Iraq, Iran has been able to send money, supplies, and personnel to support the insurgency in Iraq.

Legend:
- Iranian Commands
- Strategic distribution hubs
- Tactical distribution hubs
- Primary targets
- Command and control center

Locations shown: Baghdad, Mehran, Badrah, Al Hillah, Al Kut, Dimaniyah, Al Fajr, Amarah, Al Sheeb, Ahvaz, Samawah, Nasiriyah, Qurnah, Majnun, Basrah, Shalamcheh. Countries: IRAQ, IRAN.

Taken from: Bill Roggio, "Iran's Ramazan Corps and the Ratlines into Iraq," *The Long War Journal*, December 5, 2007.

Iran can provide military assistance to any country in the region, including Iraq, based on its war experience. In all probability the group's actions are known and directed by the Iranian regime and as such are actions of the state of Iran.

### Iran Provides Financial Assistance to Iraqi Extremists

*Political.* Iran attempts to influence Iraq's internal political situation through connections to numerous political parties and factions. Observers in Iraq note that Iran casts a wide net of influence rather than focusing on one or a few players. The Supreme Council for the Islamic Revolution in Iraq (SCIRI), Dawa, the Sadr movement, and other Shiite organizations are all reportedly in contact with Iranian operatives within Iraq—in addition to consulting with Iranian officials in Tehran. U.S. intelligence indicates that Iran is also providing financial aid to Iraqi extremist organizations. The fact that Iranian agents detained by the United States have included Quds Force personnel in a SCIRI compound and in a long-established Iranian government office in the Kurdish region underscores the scope of Iran's reported activity in Iraq.

## Iran Is Building Social and Religious Connections in Iraq

*Social.* Through the provision of social services, medical care, and support to the Shiite religious community, Iran has created a network of influence at all levels in Shiite Iraq. Some Iraqis travel to Iran for medical care unavailable in Iraq, free of charge. Iranian media extend widely across southern Iraq, including at least one television network (al-Alam).

*Religious.* Under an agreement between the two countries, 1,500 Iranian pilgrims a day cross into Iraq. That is 547,500 people a year— by far the largest group of civilian foreigners entering Iraq. Such pilgrims are a major presence in the Shia holy cities of Najaf and Karbala. As explained by Washington Institute visiting fellow Mehdi Khalaji in Policy Focus no. 59, *The Last Maria: Sistani and the End of Traditional Religious Authority in Shiism*, Iran has become a major influence on Shiite religious education circles in Iraq.

## Iran Profits from Chaos in Iraq

*Economic.* Iran has growing trade ties with Iraq, particularly, and is establishing a branch of its state bank in Baghdad. Tehran is offering assistance in reconstruction, based on its own experience of postwar rebuilding. Iranian businessmen are very active in the Kurdish region, especially around Sulaymaniyah, and throughout southern Iraq. On January 15, [2007] Iraq and Iran signed a "Memorandum of Understanding" to expand cooperation in air, land, and sea transportation. While Iran represents these activities as being beneficial to Iraq, they are arguably as beneficial to Iran; in at least several cases, Iranians seem to be profiting well from their role in Iraq. These activities also have the effect of creating a denser web of relationships between the two states.

## Iran Pretends to Be a Friend to Iraq

*Diplomatic.* Iran's leadership makes frequent public statements concerning the situation in Iraq, attempting to present itself as Iraq's friend, as supportive of Iraq's independence, and as critical of the United States and its activities in Iraq. It receives both elected Iraqi officials and factional leaders in Tehran as official guests. Muqtada al-Sadr [an influential Iraqi cleric] has made at least two visits to Iran, including one during which he pledged to use his Mahdi Army to defend Islamic states if attacked by the United States. Iranian ambassador to Iraq Hassan Kazemi Qumi, who is reportedly a senior officer in the Quds Force, has publicly stated that it is Iran's intention to expand its economic and military activity in Iraq, while denying any involvement in attacks on Americans.

## Iraq Is Vulnerable

Iran has significant capabilities for wielding influence in Iraq. These include:

*History and experience.* Both the IRGC and the Ministry of Intelligence and Security (MOIS) have extensive experience in the Kurdish region and in southern Iraq from the time of the Saddam Hussein regime. Iran provided assistance to Kurdish elements including both the Kurdistan Democratic Party (KDP) and the Patriotic Union of Kurdistan (PUK) in their struggles against Saddam, and had extensive dealings with SCIRI, Dawa, and the exiled leaders of both. Iranian operatives well know the complex human, physical, and operational terrain of Shiite Iraq.

*Appropriate military capabilities.* Chaotic and unsettled conditions in Iraq make it a good operational area for special forces and unconventional capabilities. The IRGC and Quds Force, as well as the MOIS, are well adapted for operations in Iraq. They have the skills to establish safe houses, monitor the movement of coalition forces, tend weapons caches, facilitate cross-border travel, smuggle munitions and money, and recruit individuals as intelligence sources.

*Geography.* Iraqi officials along the 870-mile Iraq-Iran border are not able to exercise serious control, and, in some cases, are complicit with smugglers. Iran probably uses both official and unofficial crossing points to move men, money, and materials into Iraq. According to

U.S. intelligence, there are three primary areas of Iranian cross-border arms smuggling: the Mandali area east of Baghdad, the Mehran area in the southern marsh region, and the Basra area.

*Surrogates and allies.* In addition to its own forces, Iran employs surrogates and allies to aid its activities in Iraq. [Political and military organization] Hizballah in Lebanon is reportedly assisting Iran by providing military and unconventional warfare training and IED technology to Shiite fighters. U.S. intelligence reports indicate that 1,000 to 2,000 militiamen had been sent to Lebanon for training as of November 2006.

*Will.* Finally, Iran has the interest and the will to carry out prolonged underground action in Iraq. It has an interest in shaping the future government and direction of Iraq, and in weakening U.S. resources and will. Tehran is capable of fighting a long war of its own, and Iraq is a good place to do it. Furthermore, at least some in the Iranian government seem to think that escalating tensions with the United States will make Washington back off from pressing Iran on its nuclear program. . . .

> **FAST FACT**
>
> A 2007 CNN/Opinion Research Corporation poll found that 82 percent of Americans believe the Iranian government is providing weapons to insurgents in Iraq.

### Iran's Leaders Willing to Take Risks in Iraq

Iran is using all means necessary to achieve its aims in Iraq. Some of these means are overt and represent the normal stuff of diplomacy and influence. Others are secret operations carried out by clandestine elements of the Iranian regime, and are intended to remain undiscovered—or at least deniable. Iran employs the Quds Force for precisely this kind of activity. The Quds Force's known presence in Iraq is itself evidence of clandestine Iranian operations. The fact that Iran's ambassador in Baghdad reportedly is a high-ranking member of the Quds Force proves the boldness—even brazen cynicism—of the Iranian regime. . . .

Iranian behavior in Iraq says something about the state and its leadership. Iran's leaders are ruthless, clever, and willing to take risks in Iraq. This should be noted and understood as Iran acts on other issues. The choices for dealing with the Iranian challenge, both in and outside Iraq, are not clear, and the consequences of making the wrong choices are dire. But by the time the choices are clear, it will be too late for anything but acquiescence [agreement without protest] to the presence of a nuclear-armed Iran driven by hostility toward the West—or a war to prevent it.

### EVALUATING THE AUTHOR'S ARGUMENTS:

Jeffrey White uses history, facts, and examples to make his argument that the United States should reserve the right to attack Iran if necessary. He does not, however, use any quotations to support his point. If you were to rewrite this article and insert quotations, what authorities might you quote from? Where would you place these quotations to bolster the points White makes?

## Viewpoint 6

# Iran Is Not Likely to Help Terrorists Attack America and Its Allies

### Ted Galen Carpenter

> *"Iran has possessed chemical weapons for decades, yet there is no indication that it has passed on any of those weapons to Hezbollah or to Palestinian groups."*

Ted Galen Carpenter argues in the following viewpoint that Iran is not likely to help terrorists attack America and its allies. Although Iran openly supports terrorist groups like Hezbollah, Carpenter does not believe Iran would give nuclear weapons to terrorists. For one, Iran has possessed chemical weapons for decades, and it has not shared these weapons with terrorist groups. But, he says, Iran is most unlikely to share nuclear weapons with terrorists because it would be afraid of how the United States and its allies would respond if it did. The United States would not stand for such behavior and would likely punish Iran severely if it discovered that Iran was the source of weapons in terrorist hands. Carpenter also points out that even Iran knows that giving terrorists nuclear weapons is a bad idea—terrorists are not loyal

Ted Galen Carpenter, "Iran's Nuclear Program; America's Policy Options," *Policy Analysis*, September 20, 2006, p. 11. Copyright © 2006 by Cato Institute. Republished with permission of the Cato Institute, conveyed through Copyright Clearance Center, Inc.

to any one state, and Iran's own weapons might be used one day to attack it. Carpenter concludes it is much more likely that Iran would keep its nuclear weapons for itself to bolster its sense of power and position in the world.

Carpenter is vice president for defense and foreign policy studies at the Cato Institute, a nonprofit public policy research foundation. He is also the author of seven books on international affairs, including *Peace and Freedom: Foreign Policy for a Constitutional Republic*.

**AS YOU READ, CONSIDER THE FOLLOWING QUESTIONS:**
1. What terrorist group does the author say Iran has a notable relationship with?
2. If Iran gave nuclear weapons to terrorists the United States would consider it an act of what, according to the author?
3. What sign does the author say Iranian leaders gave the United States in the spring of 2006 that indicates they are interested in negotiating?

Iran would be at or near the top of a list of countries Americans would least like to see have nuclear weapons, and the reasons for apprehension have deepened dramatically in [2005] with the election of President Mahmoud Ahmadinejad. Iran under the mullahs [religious leaders] since the revolution of 1979 has been a weird and ominous country. With Ahmadinejad's new prominence, the weirdness quotient has reached new levels. Iran is now headed by an individual who expresses the hope that Israel be wiped off the map and denies that the Holocaust ever occurred. Those are sentiments not found in civilized circles anywhere in the world. . . .

## Iran Would Not Share Weapons with Terrorist Groups

[Iranian capital] Tehran does have a cozy relationship with a number of terrorist organizations in the Middle East, most notably Hezbollah. The pervasive assumption among American hawks[1] is that if Iran obtains nuclear weapons, sooner or later it will pass one along to a terrorist ally.

1. Advocates of aggressive political policies.

But how likely is it that Iran would make such a transfer? At the very least, it would be an incredibly high-risk strategy. Even the most fanatical mullahs in Tehran realize that the United States would attack the probable supplier of such a weapon—and Iran would be at the top of Washington's list of suspects.

It is significant that Iran has possessed chemical weapons for decades, yet there is no indication that it has passed on any of those weapons to Hezbollah or to Palestinian groups that Tehran supports politically. Why should one assume that the mullahs would be more reckless with nuclear weapons when the prospect of devastating retaliation for an attack would be even more likely? The more logical conclusion is that Iran, like other nuclear powers, would jealously guard its arsenal.

## Iran Knows an Attack Would Not Be Tolerated

Just in case the mullahs might entertain thoughts of transferring such weaponry, though, U.S. leaders should be explicit about the

### Iran Is Unlikely to Share Nuclear Weapons with Terrorists

A poll of foreign-policy authorities revealed they think it is unlikely Iran would give nuclear weapons to terrorists.

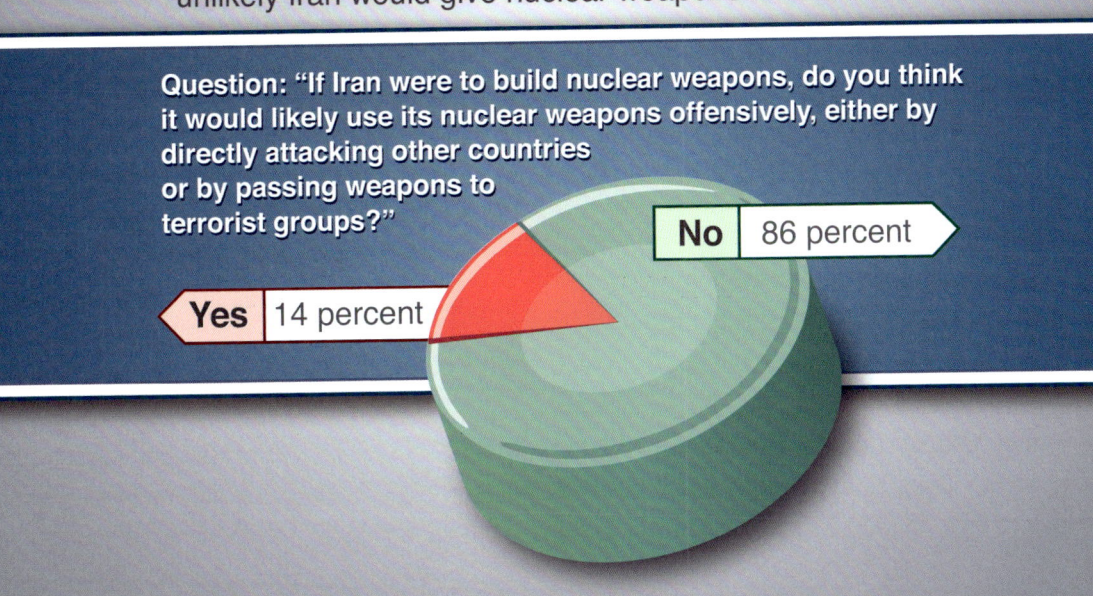

Question: "If Iran were to build nuclear weapons, do you think it would likely use its nuclear weapons offensively, either by directly attacking other countries or by passing weapons to terrorist groups?"

Yes 14 percent
No 86 percent

Taken from: "Nuclear Iran," *Atlantic*, September 2006. www.theatlantic.com/doc/200609/poll.

consequences, making it clear that such a transfer is a very bright red line that no regime can cross and hope to survive. The reason for such an uncompromising position on that point is that al-Qaeda and its ilk are not deterrable; they are not rational nation-state actors, and they have no fixed "return address" for the purposes of retaliation. The message to Tehran should be that we can tolerate Iran in the global nuclear club, albeit reluctantly, but any transfer of nuclear material or weapons to nonstate actors will be considered an act of war, and a regime-ending event. . . .

## America Should Negotiate with Iran

We should make a serious diplomatic effort to get Iran to give up its quest for nuclear weapons—and that means going substantially beyond the scope of the EU-3-led negotiations [diplomatic talks led by Britain, France, and Germany]. Washington should propose a grand bargain to Tehran. That means giving an assurance that the United States will not use force against Iran the way we did against such nonnuclear adversaries as Serbia and Iraq. It also means offering restored diplomatic relations and normal economic relations. In return, Iran would be required to open its nuclear program to unfettered international inspections to guarantee that the program is used solely for peaceful power-generation purposes. . . .

> **Fast Fact**
>
> In July 2007 the al Qaeda terrorist organization leader in Iraq, Abu Omar al-Baghdadi, issued an Internet video warning that his Sunni followers were preparing to wage war against Shiite-dominated Iran.

## Iran Reaches Out to America

There are intriguing signs that at least some portions of the clerical regime would like an improved relationship with the United States. According to the *Washington Post*, the Iranian government approached the Bush administration in 2002—after Bush's hostile "Axis of Evil" comment in his State of the Union address—and proposed cooperating with the United States against Al Qaeda. As a gesture of good faith, they informed Washington of the identities of 290 members of

*An Iranian man reads news of Iranian president Ahmadinejad's letter to President George W. Bush in 2006. Many consider the letter a move to reach out to the United States.*

Al Qaeda that Iran had captured and sent back to their home countries. The Bush administration spurned that overture. Aides to Vice President Dick Cheney and Secretary of Defense Donald Rumsfeld argued that any diplomatic engagement would "legitimate" Iran and other state sponsors of terrorism.

In the spring of 2006 Ahmadinejad surprised Washington and the rest of the international community by sending a lengthy letter to President George Bush—the first communication to an American chief executive from an Iranian head of state in decades. It was a curious document—a rambling 18-page treatise on history, religion, politics, and world affairs. As a foundation for serious, substantive negotiations on the Iranian nuclear crisis, the letter was decidedly inadequate. Nevertheless, it was a sign that even the hardest of the Iranian hardliners was interested in some dialogue with Washington.

Ahmadinejad's letter was not the only feeler for negotiations. A few days later, *Time* magazine published an open letter from Hassan Rohani, representative of Iran's Supreme Leader, Ayatollah Ali Khameini. That letter was considerably more focused and substantive than Ahmadinejad's missive. The former speaker of the Iranian parliament, Mehdi Karroubi, has been perhaps the boldest of all in favoring a rapprochement with the United States. "This silence between the two countries cannot go on forever," he said. "The ice should be broken and the walls of mistrust should fall."

## A Grand Bargain

Although those initiatives may have been a factor that finally induced Washington to join the EU-3-led negotiations with Tehran, U.S. leaders still avoid any suggestion of bilateral negotiations with the Iranian government. Indeed, Secretary of State [Condoleeza] Rice went out of her way to stress that U.S. participation in the multilateral talks in no way implied that Washington was willing to consider a grand bargain. That attitude needs to change. Bilateral negotiations will be necessary to pursue the strategy of a grand bargain, because the United States holds most of the carrots that Iran desires. The European powers (and Russia and China) might be able to facilitate such negotiations, but progress will be unlikely unless there are direct talks between Tehran and Washington.

And we have little to lose by making the offer of a grand bargain—unless we were to let negotiations drag on endlessly. Proposing the grand bargain to Tehran and indicating that the offer would remain on the table for a maximum of six months would have no significant downside. If the Iranians rejected the proposal—or if they simply stalled—. . . other options would still be available.

## EVALUATING THE AUTHOR'S ARGUMENTS:

One of Carpenter's arguments is that Iran would not give nuclear weapons to terrorists because in the past it has not given them other types of weapons. Does this kind of reasoning appeal to you? Do you think it is reasonable to assume that if Iran were going to give weapons of mass destruction to terrorists, it would have done so by now? Explain what your position is, and why.

# Chapter 2

# Is Iran Developing Nuclear Weapons?

*According to the National Council of Resistance, this picture shows clandestine development of nuclear weapons at an Iranian nuclear facility.*

# Viewpoint 1

# Iran Is Probably Developing Weapons of Mass Destruction

*"The U.S. Intelligence Community assesses that Iran is intent on developing a nuclear weapons capability."*

**U.S. House of Representatives Permanent Select Committee on Intelligence, Subcommittee on Intelligence Policy**

In the following viewpoint the U.S. House of Represeratives Permanent Select Committee on Intelligence, Subcommittee on Intelligence Policy, argues that Iran is most likely developing weapons of mass destruction. Iranian leaders claim that Iran is pursuing nuclear technology to generate electricity for its people. But the authors say ample evidence indicates that Iran intends to make nuclear weapons. The authors show that Iran is enriching uranium to weapons-grade levels and is producing small quantities of plutonium. Furthermore, other actions taken by Iran, such as its reluctance to cooperate with the International Atomic Energy Agency, and the fact that it has large oil and

House Permanent Select Committee on Intelligence, Subcommittee on Intelligence Policy, "Recognizing Iran as a Strategic Threat: An Intelligence Challenge for the United States," *Staff Report of the House Permanent Select Committee on Intelligence, Subcommittee on Intelligence Policy,* U. S. House of Representatives, August 23, 2006. Public Domain.

natural gas supplies and has no need for nuclear energy, indicate that Iran intends to build nuclear weapons, not nuclear power. Furthermore, if Iran were developing a peaceful nuclear program it would have no reason to hide it. Given these facts, the authors conclude that Iran is probably making nuclear weapons.

The U.S. House of Representatives Permanent Select Committee on Intelligence, Subcommittee on Intelligence Policy oversees the legislative aspects of U.S. intelligence policy.

**AS YOU READ, CONSIDER THE FOLLOWING QUESTIONS:**
1. According to the authors, what is the main process by which Iran is producing fissile material for nuclear weapons?
2. How many tons of uranium hexafluoride do the authors say Iran has produced?
3. What three things make the authors think Iran's nuclear program is probably not for peaceful purposes?

Two decades ago, Iran embarked on a secret program to acquire the capability to produce weapons-grade nuclear material. Iran has developed an extensive infrastructure, from laboratories to industrial facilities, to support its research for nuclear weapons. Producing fissile material is a complicated process and Tehran [the Iranian capital] faces several key obstacles to acquiring a nuclear capability: its inability to produce or purchase fissile [capable of nuclear fission] material, the challenges of marrying a nuclear warhead to a missile, and the difficulty of adjusting its existing missiles to carry a nuclear payload.

Since 2002, the IAEA [International Atomic Energy Agency] has issued a series of reports detailing how Iran has covertly engaged in dozens of nuclear-related activities that violate its treaty obligations[1] to openly cooperate with the IAEA. These activities included false statements to IAEA inspectors, carrying out certain nuclear activities and experiments without notifying the IAEA, and numerous steps to deceive and mislead the IAEA.

---

1. Iran signed the Nuclear Non-proliferation Treaty in 1970.

## Iran's Nuclear Weapons Program

The principal method Iran is pursuing at this time to produce fissile material for nuclear weapons is a process known as uranium enrichment. This method involves spinning gaseous uranium hexafluoride ($UF_6$) in large numbers of centrifuge machines to increase the fraction of uranium-235 (U-235), the uranium isotope that can be used as weapons fuel. Naturally occurring uranium contains only a very small fraction of this isotope (0.71%), thus the need for the enrichment process. Weapons-grade uranium contains about 90% U-235.

The IAEA has also uncovered evidence that Iran has pursued another route for nuclear weapons by producing plutonium. Plutonium can be separated from irradiated nuclear material such as "spent" fuel rods from a nuclear power reactor. North Korea is believed to have produced plutonium for nuclear weapons by separating plutonium from spent fuel rods. . . .

## The United States Is in the Dark

The WMD Commission (officially known as the Commission on the Intelligence of the United States Regarding Weapons of Mass Destruction) concluded in its March 2005 unclassified report that "across the board, the Intelligence Community knows disturbingly little about the nuclear programs of many of the world's most dangerous actors." American intelligence agencies do not know nearly enough about Iran's nuclear weapons program. However, based on what is known about Iranian behavior and Iranian deception efforts, the U.S. Intelligence Community assesses that Iran is intent on developing a nuclear weapons capability. Publicly available information also leads to the conclusion that Iran has a nuclear weapons program, especially taking into account the following facts:

- Iran has covertly pursued two parallel enrichment programs—a laser process based on Russian technology and a centrifuge process. The Russian government terminated cooperation with Iran on laser enrichment in 2001, following extensive consultations with the United States, and it appears to be no longer active.
- In February 2004, Iran admitted to obtaining uranium centrifuge technology on the black market shortly after Dr. A.Q. Khan, the father of Pakistan's nuclear weapons program, confessed to secretly

# Iran's Nuclear Sites

Iran is believed to have many facilities dedicated to the creation of nuclear weapons.

**Mo-Allem Kalayeh:** Suspected nuclear research center

**Karaj:** Cyclon accelerator research

**Tehran:**
Kalaye Electric: enrichment
Nuclear Research Center
Sharif University research
Atomic Energy of Iran

**Bonab:** Research and development

**Chalus:** Weapons development facility

**Jabr Iban Hagan:** Research and conversion

**Gorgan:** Research facilities

**Tabriz:** Engineering defense research

**Damarand:** Plasma physics research

**Ramandeh:** Uranium enrichment

**Natanz:** Enrichment facility

**Lashkar-Abad:** Uranium enrichment

**Esfahan:** Nuclear research facilities

**Khondab:** Heavy water plant

**Saghand:** Uranium mine

**Arak:** Heavy water reactor

**Darkhouin:** Suspected uranium enrichment site

**Ardakan:** Uranium ore purification

**Bushehr:** Light water nuclear reactor

**Fasa:** Uranium conversion

**Yazd:** Milling plant

**Narigan:** Uranium mine

**Zarigan:** Uranium mine

Taken from: Nuclear Threat Initiative, 2006.

providing this technology to Iran, Libya, and North Korea. Khan also sold nuclear bomb plans to Libya. It is not known whether Khan sold nuclear weapon plans to Iran.

## Discoveries by the IAEA

- The IAEA reported on February 27, 2006, that Iran has produced approximately 85 tons of uranium hexafluoride ($UF_6$). If enriched through centrifuges to weapons-grade material—a capability Iran is working hard to master—this would be enough for 12 nuclear bombs.
- To produce plutonium, Iran has built a heavy water production plant and is constructing a large, heavy water–moderated reactor whose technical characteristics are well-suited for the production of weapons-grade plutonium. In support of this effort, Iran admitted in October 2003 to secretly producing small quantities of plutonium without notifying the IAEA, a violation of its treaty obligations.
- The IAEA has discovered documentation in Iran for casting and machining enriched uranium hemispheres, which are directly relevant to production of nuclear weapons components. The IAEA is also pursuing information on nuclear-related high-explosive tests and the design of a delivery system, both of which point to a military rather than peaceful purpose of the Iranian nuclear program.
- The IAEA discovered evidence in September 2003 that Iran had covertly produced the short-lived radioactive element polonium 210 (Po-210), a substance with two known uses: a neutron source for a nuclear weapon and satellite batteries. Iran told the IAEA that the polonium 210 was produced for satellite batteries but could not produce evidence for this explanation. The IAEA found Iran's explanation about its polonium experiments difficult to believe, stating in a September 2004 report that "it remains, however, somewhat uncertain regarding the plausibility of the stated purpose of the experiments given the very limited applications of short lived Po-210 sources."

## Timeline to an Iranian Nuclear Bomb

The U.S. Intelligence Community believes Iran could have a nuclear weapon sometime in the beginning to the middle of the next decade. The timetable for an Iranian program depends on a wide range of factors—such as the acquisition of key components and materials, successful testing, outside assistance (if any), and the impact of domestic and international political pressures. It also depends on the assumption that Iran will overcome technical hurdles to master the technology at some point and that its leaders will not be deterred from developing nuclear weapons in the interim.

Increasing its number of centrifuges will dramatically decrease the time required for Iran to produce sufficient fissile material for a nuclear weapon. Former Iranian President Rafsanjani said on April 11, 2006 that Iran was producing enriched uranium in a small, 164-centrifuge cascade using "P-1" centrifuge technology, a basic Pakistani centrifuge design. Iran announced in April 2006 that it plans to build a 3,000-centrifuge cascade by early 2007 and ultimately plans to construct a 54,000 centrifuge cascade. . . .

## Iran's Nuclear Program Is Not for Peaceful Purposes

Iran has engaged in an extensive campaign to conceal from the IAEA and the world the true nature of its nuclear program.

Iran claims that its nuclear program is peaceful and for civilian electricity. While there are differences among some experts as to

*Iranian president Ahmadinejad tours one of his country's nuclear facilities, inspecting the centrifuges on display. The authors argue that such facilities are geared toward making nuclear weapons, not nuclear power.*

whether Iran may have an interest in a civilian nuclear program in addition to a weapons program, recent findings by the Department of Energy make a convincing case that that the Iranian nuclear program is inconsistent with the Iranian Government's stated purpose of developing civil nuclear power in order to achieve energy independence. Iran's claims that its nuclear program is peaceful also is belied [shown to be false] by its record of non-cooperation with the IAEA, its decision to pursue nuclear technology covertly, and the fact that Iran does not have enough indigenous uranium resources to fuel even one power-generating reactor over its lifetime, although it does have enough uranium to make several nuclear bombs.

## Fast Fact

The U.S. national intelligence estimate confirmed in November 2007 the existence of a covert Iranian program to develop nuclear weapons, as well as missiles capable of delivering them.

Aside from Iran's lack of uranium deposits, Iran's claim that its nuclear program is for electricity production appears doubtful in light of its large oil and natural gas reserves. Iran's natural gas reserves are the second largest in the world and the energy industry estimates that Iran flares enough natural gas annually to generate electricity equivalent to the output of four Bushehr reactors.[2] . . .

Furthermore, there is no rational reason for Iran to pursue a peaceful nuclear program in secret and risk international sanctions when the International Atomic Energy Agency encourages and assists peaceful nuclear programs. If Iran sincerely wanted a peaceful nuclear program, the IAEA would have helped it develop one provided that Tehran agreed to IAEA supervision and monitoring.

## Iran Continues to Conceal Its Nuclear Activities

In an October 1, 2003 agreement with the EU-3 [the United Kingdom, France, and Germany], Iran pledged "to engage in full cooperation with the IAEA to address and resolve through full transparency all requirements and outstanding issues of the Agency." In spite of this, Iran has

---

2. A nuclear reactor located at a nuclear facility in Bushehr, Iran.

admitted to conducting certain nuclear activities to IAEA inspectors only after the IAEA presented it with clear evidence or asked Tehran to correct prior explanations that were inaccurate, implausible, or fraught with contradictions. Iran's admissions have been grudging and piecemeal, and its cooperation with IAEA inspectors has been accompanied by protests, accusations, and threats. Iran's recalcitrant behavior toward IAEA inspections drove IAEA Director Mohamed ElBaradei to declare in a November 2003 report:

> The recent disclosures by Iran about its nuclear program clearly show that, in the past, Iran had concealed many aspects of its nuclear activities, with resultant breaches of its obligation to comply with the provisions of the Safeguards Agreement. Iran's policy of concealment continued until last month, with co-operation being limited and reactive, and information being slow in coming, changing and contradictory. . . .

## Iran Must Be Discouraged from Developing Nuclear Weapons

It is vital that the Intelligence Community also provide intelligence the United States can use to prevent Iran from acquiring WMD technology and materials. This is a global challenge and the U.S. Intelligence Community must be prepared to play an important role as the Administration seeks the cooperation of like-minded government officials in efforts to prevent Iran from acquiring WMD or discouraging the Iranian regime and people from continuing to pursue such programs.

**EVALUATING THE AUTHORS' ARGUMENTS:**

In this viewpoint the authors argue that Iran is developing enough uranium for as many as twelve nuclear bombs. How do you think the author of the following viewpoint, Juan Cole, might respond to this claim? In your answer, list the evidence each viewpoint provides to prove its case.

**Viewpoint 2**

# Iran Is Probably Not Developing Nuclear Weapons

## Juan Cole

*"The only thing that the IAEA knows for sure is that Iran has a peaceful nuclear energy research program. Such a program is not the same as a weapons program."*

In the following viewpoint Juan Cole argues that no evidence supports the view that Iran is developing nuclear weapons. He explains that for years, the United States has claimed that Iran wants nuclear weapons and is aggressively pursuing a nuclear weapons program. But Cole says the United States has bad intelligence on Iran's nuclear program. Cole claims that Iran is developing a peaceful nuclear energy program. In fact, according to Cole, Iran does not have the materials to enrich enough uranium to make even one nuclear bomb. Nor does it have the missiles needed to launch a nuclear attack. Furthermore, the International Atomic Energy Agency has stated that Iran has complied with the Nuclear Non-proliferation Treaty. Cole says the United States was wrong about Iraq having weapons of mass destruction in 2003, and thus is also probably wrong about Iran having nuclear weapons.

Juan Cole, "Folks, We Are Being Set Up Again! Iran's Nuclear Threat," *CounterPunch,* August 25, 2006. Reproduced by permission.

Cole is president of the Global Americana Institute, a nonprofit organization dedicated to bridging the gap of misunderstanding between the United States and the Arab world. One of its programs involves translating key works of American history and thought into Arabic.

**AS YOU READ, CONSIDER THE FOLLOWING QUESTIONS:**
1. According to Cole, how many centrifuges does it take to enrich enough uranium to make a nuclear bomb? How many centrifuges does Iran have?
2. Under what treaty is Iran's energy program legal, according to the author?
3. What long-range missile does the author say that Iran does *not* have in its possession?

Here is what the professionals are saying about the Republican-dominated Subcommittee on Intelligence Policy report on Iran that slams US intelligence professionals for poor intelligence on Iran: The report demonstrates that these Republicans have poor intelligence . . . on Iran. What follows is summaries of things I've seen from other experts but I can't identify them without permission.

### U.S. Intelligence Officials Are Not Qualified

First of all, former CIA professionals Larry Johnson and Jim Marcinkowski point out that the Republicans have a lot of damn gall. It was high members of this Republican administration who leaked to the Iranians and the whole world the name of Valerie Plame, an undercover CIA operative who spent her professional career combatting the proliferation of WMD [weapons of mass destruction] and was, at the time she was betrayed by Traitor Rove [Karl Rove, deputy chief of staff to President George W. Bush] and his merry band, working on Iran. Had it not been for these Republican figures, none of whom has yet been punished in any way for endangering US national security, we might know more about Iran.

It is being said that the staffer who headed the report is Frederick Fleitz, who was a special assistant to John Bolton when Bolton was undersecretary of state for proliferation issues. Fleitz was sent to the unemployment line when Condi [Secretary of State Condoleeza Rice] wisely exiled Bolton to the United Nations, where there is a long history of ill-tempered despots who like to bang their shoes on the podium. So this report is the long arm of Bolton popping up in Congress. It is Neoconservative propaganda.

I repeat what I have said before, which is that John Bolton is just an ill-tempered lawyer who has no special expertise in nuclear issues or in Iran, and aside from an ability to scare the bejesus out of young gofers who bring him coffee and to thunderously denounce on cue

## Nuclear Power or Nuclear Weapons?

Nuclear energy generation and nuclear weapons development involve many of the same steps. This makes it difficult for inspectors to tell whether Iran is developing nuclear technology for peaceful or military purposes.

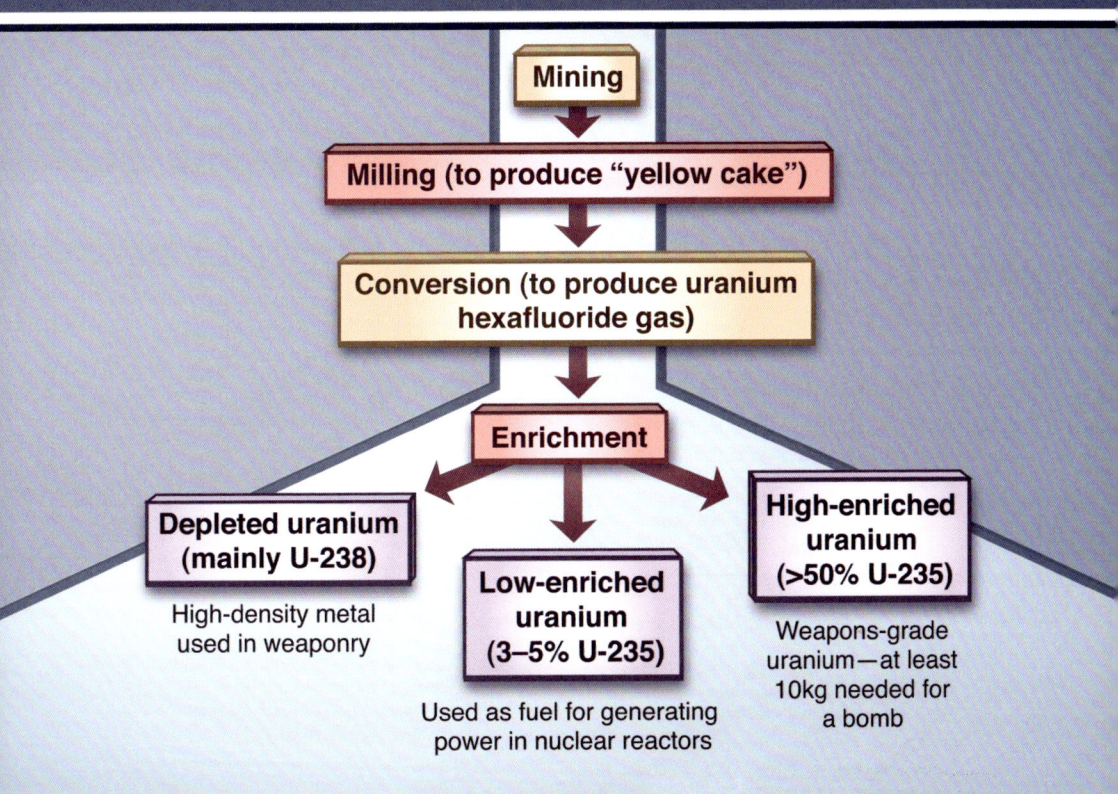

Mining
↓
Milling (to produce "yellow cake")
↓
Conversion (to produce uranium hexafluoride gas)
↓
Enrichment
↓

**Depleted uranium (mainly U-238)**
High-density metal used in weaponry

**Low-enriched uranium (3–5% U-235)**
Used as fuel for generating power in nuclear reactors

**High-enriched uranium (>50% U-235)**
Weapons-grade uranium—at least 10kg needed for a bomb

Taken from: British Broadcasting Company.

any world leader on whom he is sicced, he has no particular qualifications for his job.

## Intelligence Officials Have Been Wrong
Nor do the Republican congressmen know anything special about Iran's nuclear energy program. They certainly know much less than the CIA agents who work on it full time, some of whom know Persian and have actually done . . . intelligence work.

We are beset by instant experts on contemporary Iran, like the medievalist Bernard Lewis, who wrongly predicted that Iranian President Mahmoud Ahmadinejad would attack Israel on August 22 [2006], based on Lewis's weird interpretation of his alleged millenarian [apocalyptic] beliefs. Once the Neoconservatives went so far as actually to make fun of reality in the hearing of a reporter, their game was up.

> **FAST FACT**
> In October 2007 Mohamed ElBaradei of the International Atomic Energy Agency reported the IAEA had seen "no evidence" that Iran was developing nuclear weapons.

Pete Hoekstra, who is the chair of this committee, has a long history of saying things that are disconnected from reality. Like when he made a big deal about some old shells with mustard gas found in Iraq left over from the 1980s Iran-Iraq War, and claimed that these were the fabled and long-sought Iraqi WMD over which 2600 of our service people are six feet under and another 8000 in wheelchairs. Nope.

Bolton at one point was exercised about an imaginary Cuban biological weapons program, which even his own staffers wouldn't support him on, and at one point he was alleging that Iranian mullahs [religious leaders] were sneaking into Havana to help with it.

## Iran Does Not Have Enough Uranium to Make a Bomb
This congressional report is full of the same sort of wild fantasies.

On page 9, the report alleges that "Iran is currently enriching uranium to weapons grade using a 164-machine centrifuge cascade at this facility in Natanz."

This is an outright lie. Enriching to weapons grade would require at least 80% enrichment. Iran claims . . . 2.5 percent. See how that isn't the same thing? See how you can't blow up anything with 2.5 percent?

The claim is not only flat wrong, but it is misleading in another way. You need 16,000 centrifuges, hooked up so that they cascade, to make enough enriched uranium for a bomb in any realistic time

*In March 2003 International Atomic Energy Agency head Mohamed ElBaradei tells reporters that no evidence of a nuclear weapons program was found in Iraq. In the author's opinion, there is no reason to suspect that one exists in Iran, either.*

frame, even if you know how to get the 80 percent! Iran has . . . 164. See how that isn't the same?

The report cites the International Atomic Energy Agency [IAEA] only when it is critical of Iran. It does not tell us what the IAEA actually has found.

## The United States Was Wrong About Iraq and Is Probably Wrong About Iran

By the way, here is what IAEA head Mohamed Elbaradei said in early March, 2003, about Iraq:

> After three months of intrusive inspections, we have to date found no evidence or plausible indication of the revival of a nuclear weapons programme in Iraq.

At the same time, Republicans like [then secretary of defense] Donald Rumsfeld were saying he knew exactly where Iraq's WMD was!

Elbaradei was right then, and Fleitz was wrong. Can't get fooled again.

## Iran Has Obeyed the Nonproliferation Treaty

And here is what the IAEA said about Iran just last January [2006]:

> Iran has continued to facilitate access under its Safeguards Agreement as requested by the Agency, and to act as if the Additional Protocol is in force, including by providing in a timely manner the requisite declarations and access to locations.

Last April [2006] Elbaradei complained about the hype around Iran's nuclear research, and said that there is no imminent threat from Iran.

The only thing that the IAEA knows for sure is that Iran has a peaceful nuclear energy research program. Such a program is not the same as a weapons program, and it is perfectly legal under the Nonproliferation Treaty, which Iran, unlike Israel, has actually signed.

## Iran Is Not a Nuclear Threat

The report allegedly vastly exaggerates the range of Iran's missiles and also exaggerates the number of its longer-range ones, and seems to think that Iran already has the Shahab-4, which it does not. It also doesn't seem to realize that Iran can't send missiles on other countries without receiving them back. Israel has more and longer-range missiles than Iran, and can quickly equip them with real nuclear warheads, not the imaginary variety in Fleitz's fevered brain.

Folks, we are being set up again.

> **EVALUATING THE AUTHOR'S ARGUMENTS:**
>
> The author of this viewpoint, Juan Cole, is highly critical of U.S. intelligence officials and their ability to determine whether Iran is actually developing weapons of mass destruction. Describe some of the language Cole uses to characterize these officials. In your opinion, do these harsh words add or detract from his argument? Explain what you think, and why.

# Viewpoint 3

# The United States Should Prevent Iran from Getting Nuclear Technology

### American Israel Public Affairs Committee

*"The United States should dramatically increase efforts to prevent Iran from acquiring sensitive [nuclear] technologies via third countries."*

In the following viewpoint the American Israel Public Affairs Committee argues that the United States must prevent Iran from developing nuclear weapons. It argues that Iran is a dangerous and hostile nation—and it will only become more dangerous if it is allowed to acquire nuclear weapons. The committee says that the United States can prevent a nuclear Iran from becoming reality by imposing international sanctions on it. For example, it says the United States should cut off money from Iran by preventing foreign countries from investing in its oil and gas production. It also suggests imposing economic sanctions against Iran's central bank, which has been accused of sponsoring terrorism as well as Iran's nuclear weapons program. Finally, the United States should

American Israel Public Affairs Committee, "U.S. Should Do More to Prevent Nuclear-Armed Iran," May 2, 2008. www.aipac.org. Reproduced by permission.

add more surveillance to port cities that traffic goods to and from Iran. The committee concludes that these sanctions would severely limit Iran's economic resources and ability to develop nuclear weapons.

The American Israel Public Affairs Committee (AIPAC) is a pro-Israel group that works with political leaders to develop public policy that strengthens the relationship between Israel and the United States. AIPAC has worked with the U.S. Congress on various issues, including securing foreign aid for Israel and attempting to stop Iran's nuclear power program.

**AS YOU READ, CONSIDER THE FOLLOWING QUESTIONS:**
1. How many centrifuges does the author say Iran has begun installing at its Natanz uranium enrichment facility?
2. According to the author, what is the name of the Iranian bank that funds terrorism and finances Iran's nuclear weapons proliferation activities?
3. What country does the author say has become a major hub for transporting nuclear technologies to and from Iran?

Iran poses a major threat to the United States and our allies as it continues to advance its uranium enrichment capability in defiance of international law. Faced with the prospect of a nuclear-armed Iran, the United States should move quickly to implement measures that could have a major impact on efforts to prevent such a dire scenario. The United States should use existing law to sanction foreign companies investing more than $20 million in Iran's oil and gas sector, sanction Iran's central bank and foreign companies doing business with sanctioned Iranian entities, and cut off the flow of sensitive technologies to Iran.

## Iran Is Developing a Nuclear Weapons Program

*Iran continues to advance its nuclear program in direct violation of international law.*

Iran's recent announcement that it has begun installing 6,000 more centrifuges at its Natanz uranium enrichment facility represents a serious escalation of Tehran's illicit nuclear program. If Iran masters the ability to operate the 6,000 centrifuges—in addition to the more than 3,000 it currently has running—it could produce enough highly enriched uranium for one to three nuclear weapons a year.

At the same time, Iran is testing advanced P-2 centrifuges, which are capable of enriching uranium at two to five times the speed of older models.

The U.N. [United Nations] Security Council has passed three resolutions demanding that Iran suspend its uranium enrichment activity. The resolutions, passed, under Chapter VII of the U.N. charter, are the highest form of international law.

*The author points to numerous United Nations resolutions against Iran demanding it suspend its nuclear weapons program, the latest being a unanimous 14-0 decision on March 3, 2008.*

[U.S.] Secretary of Defense Robert Gates recently said he believes that Iran is pursuing a nuclear weapons program, saying in his judgment Iran is "hell-bent on acquiring nuclear weapons."

## The United States Should Prevent Money from Reaching Iran

*The United States should implement existing law and sanction foreign energy companies investing in Iran's energy sector.*

The United States has not imposed sanctions on a dozen foreign companies that have invested more than $20 million in Iran's energy sector despite the prohibition of such investment under the Iran Sanctions Act (ISA). While the law has discouraged many foreign companies from investing in Iran, other firms, seeing that no sanctions have been imposed, continue to seek major investments in Iran's oil and gas sector.

> **FAST FACT**
>
> The Nuclear Threat Initiative (NTI) estimates that by 2010, Iran's ballistic missiles will be able to reach southern Europe, North Africa, and South Asia. By 2015 they are expected to have missiles capable of reaching the United States.

In filings with the [U.S.] Securities and Exchange Commission, many companies publicly disclose investments in Iran and the risk they potentially face from U.S. sanctions. France's Total, Norway's StatoilHydro, and Britain's Royal Dutch Shell in their 2007 annual reports disclose investments that violate the law.

Additionally, a number of states have passed laws to divest their pension holdings from these companies investing more than $20 million in the oil and gas sector. Several states, including Florida and Colorado, have already published lists of companies investing beyond this threshold.

The House of Representatives [in 2007] overwhelmingly passed the Iran Counter-Proliferation Act, closing the loophole in ISA that has allowed companies to avoid sanctions. The Senate should pass similar legislation it is considering and the president should sign the bill into law.

# Iranian Nuclear Time Line

Iran has been trying to acquire nuclear technology since the 1960s.

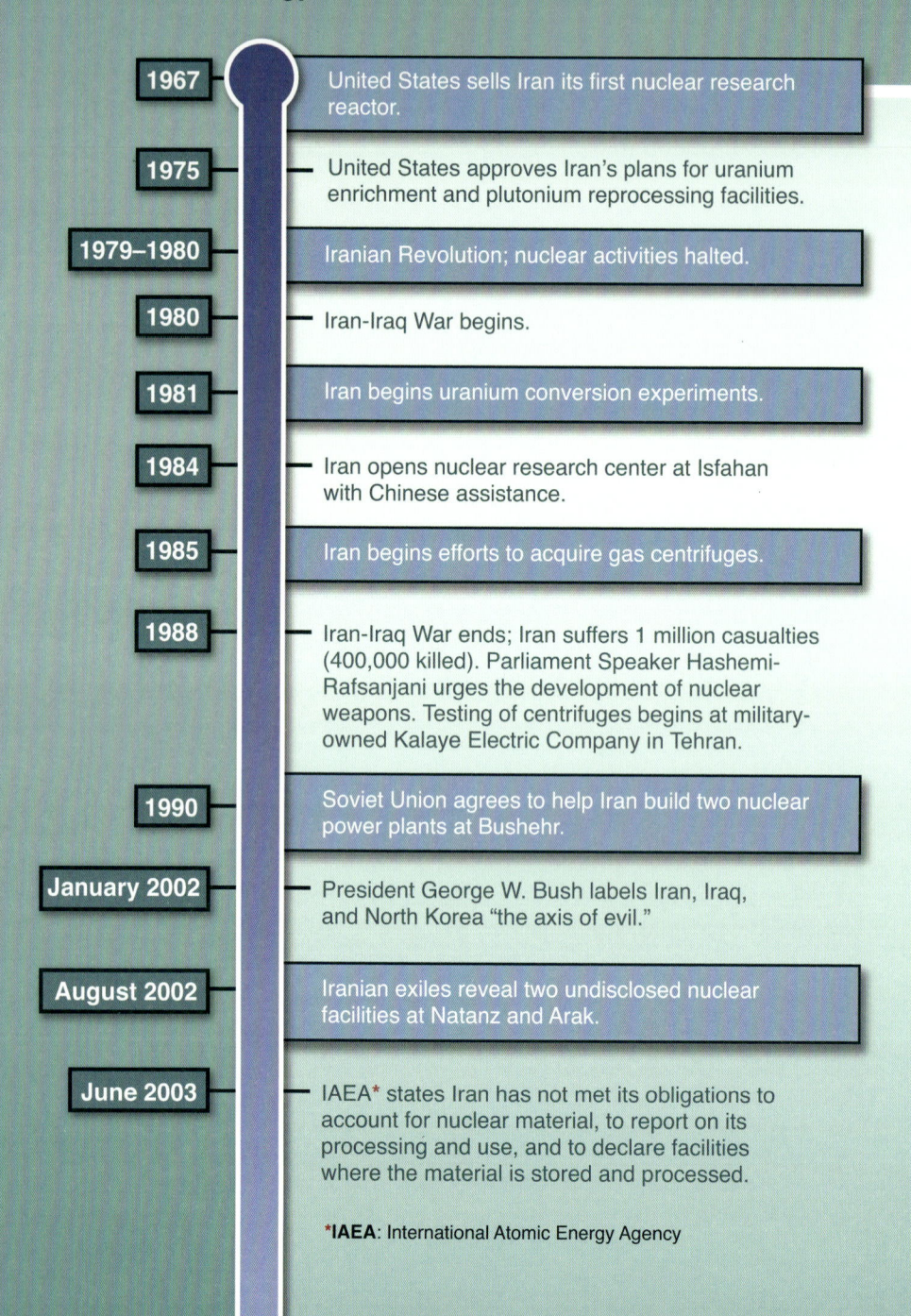

|  |  |
|---|---|
| 1967 | United States sells Iran its first nuclear research reactor. |
| 1975 | United States approves Iran's plans for uranium enrichment and plutonium reprocessing facilities. |
| 1979–1980 | Iranian Revolution; nuclear activities halted. |
| 1980 | Iran-Iraq War begins. |
| 1981 | Iran begins uranium conversion experiments. |
| 1984 | Iran opens nuclear research center at Isfahan with Chinese assistance. |
| 1985 | Iran begins efforts to acquire gas centrifuges. |
| 1988 | Iran-Iraq War ends; Iran suffers 1 million casualties (400,000 killed). Parliament Speaker Hashemi-Rafsanjani urges the development of nuclear weapons. Testing of centrifuges begins at military-owned Kalaye Electric Company in Tehran. |
| 1990 | Soviet Union agrees to help Iran build two nuclear power plants at Bushehr. |
| January 2002 | President George W. Bush labels Iran, Iraq, and North Korea "the axis of evil." |
| August 2002 | Iranian exiles reveal two undisclosed nuclear facilities at Natanz and Arak. |
| June 2003 | IAEA* states Iran has not met its obligations to account for nuclear material, to report on its processing and use, and to declare facilities where the material is stored and processed. |

*IAEA: International Atomic Energy Agency

|  |  |
|---|---|
| October 2003 | Iran begins tests on a 164-centrifuge cascade at Natanz. Iran agrees to suspend enrichment activities after talks with France, Germany, and the United Kingdom. |
| September 2004 | Iran announces plans to convert 40 tons of uranium to uranium hexafluoride ($UF_6$). |
| November 2004 | Iran signs the Paris Accord with EU-3** promising a suspension of enrichment activities in exchange for security, political, and economic assurances. |
| August 2005 | Mahmoud Ahmadinejad assumes the presidency of Iran. Days later, Iran resumes its uranium conversion program at the Isfahan nuclear complex. |
| September 2005 | IAEA Board of Governors passes resolution reporting Iranian noncompliance with NPT*** safeguards agreement. |
| April 2006 | President Ahmadinejad announces that Iran has enriched uranium to reactor-grade levels. |
| June 2006 | UN Security Council adopts Resolution 1696 giving Iran a new deadline of August 31, 2006, to comply with Security Council requests or face stronger council action. |
| October 2006 | Iran steps up its nuclear program and opens second 164-centrifuge cascade. |
| December 2006 | UN Security Council adopts Resolution 1737 imposing sanctions on Iran for failure to halt uranium enrichment. |
| February 2007 | Iran ignores a February 24, 2007, UN Security Council deadline to halt its nuclear development program. |
| 2015 | U.S. intelligence estimate of when Iran could acquire nuclear weapons capability. |

**EU-3: United Kingdom, France, and Germany
***NPT: Non-proliferation (of nuclear weapons) Treaty

Taken from: Joseph Cirincione and Andrew Grotto, "Contain and Engage: A New Strategy for Resolving the Nuclear Crisis with Iran," Center for American Progress, March 2007.

## The United States Should Sanction Iran's Central Bank

*The United States should sanction the Central Bank of Iran and any foreign company conducting business with Iranian entities under U.S. sanction.*

The Central Bank of Iran, also known as Bank Markazi, is heavily involved in the funding of terrorism and the financing of Iran's proliferation activities. The United States should designate the Central Bank as a weapons proliferator or terror supporter under existing executive orders.

The Central Bank is increasingly handling transactions for Iranian banks already designated under U.S. sanctions. Central Bank Governor Tahmasb Mazaheri said on February 5, 2007, that "the central bank assists Iranian private and state-owned banks to do their commitments regardless of the pressure on them." Sanctioning the Central Bank—Iran's principal remaining link to the international banking system—would have a dramatic effect on Iran's ability to conduct international business.

The United States should sanction foreign banks that continue to conduct transactions with the four state-owned Iranian banks subject to U.S. or U.N. sanctions. The United States should also sanction foreign entities that continue to do business with the Iranian Islamic Revolutionary Guard Corps in violation of U.S. sanctions law.

## Iran Must Be Stopped

*The United States should increase efforts to stop the flow of technologies to the United Arab Emirates (UAE) and elsewhere that end up in Iran.*

The United States should dramatically increase efforts to prevent Iran from acquiring sensitive technologies via third countries, specifically from the UAE, which has become a major hub for the illegal transshipment of goods to and from Iran. Since 2005, six distinct schemes to ship industrial products from the U.S. to Iran via the UAE were prevented or discovered after the fact.

The transfer of nuclear-grade graphite—a key material needed for the manufacture of a nuclear bomb—was stopped in October 2007 by alert customs agents in India as it was about to be shipped to the UAE and then on to Iran, according to a recent report in *The Times of India*.

The United States currently has only one export control officer stationed in the UAE. The Dubai port, one of several in the UAE, is the seventh largest container port in the world, handling the equivalent of 10.65 million standard 20-foot cargo containers in 2007.

> **EVALUATING THE AUTHOR'S ARGUMENTS:**
>
> In this viewpoint the author lays out an action plan for the United States to prevent Iran from acquiring nuclear technology. Name three of these actions. Then, state whether you think these actions can stop Iran from acquiring nuclear weapons. Or, do you think Iran will find other ways to develop its nuclear program? Explain your answer using evidence from the text.

# Viewpoint 4

# The United States Has No Right to Prevent Iran from Getting Nuclear Technology

## S. Sam Shoamanesh

*"Iran is being forced to forfeit its [in]alienable right to peaceful nuclear energy."*

The United States has no right to prevent Iran from obtaining nuclear energy, argues S. Sam Shoamanesh in the following viewpoint. He criticizes the United States for insisting that Iran plans to use its nuclear power program to develop weapons. Shoamanesh says no credible evidence proves that Iran plans to develop nuclear weapons or to use such weapons to attack the United States and its allies. In fact, Shoamanesh explains, since 1970 Iran has complied with international law pertaining to nuclear energy. Furthermore, he says, the United States has no right to interfere in Iran's pursuit of peaceful nuclear technologies, especially when the United States has

S. Sam Shoamanesh, "Iran's Nuclear Dilemma—Understanding the Iranian Threat: The Other Side of the Coin," *Harvard International Review*, October 22, 2008. Reproduced by permission of *Harvard International Review*.

one of the largest nuclear programs—both peaceful and military—in the world. The author concludes that Iran, as a sovereign nation, has every right to develop nuclear power, and the United States cannot tell it what to do.

Shoamanesh is an international lawyer and has worked both for the United Nations' International Criminal Tribunal and for its International Court of Justice.

**AS YOU READ, CONSIDER THE FOLLOWING QUESTIONS:**
1. What event does Shoamanesh say caused the West to stop supporting Iran's nuclear program?
2. According to the author, through 2005 how many days of on-site inspections had been conducted at Iran's nuclear power sites? What did these inspections yield?
3. What nuclear program does the author say Iran has offered to renounce? What effect would this have on its ability to build nuclear bombs?

Filling the void left by the collapse of Saddam Hussein's rule in Iraq and strengthened by the apparent failure of the United States' "remaking" of the Middle East project in the aftermath of 9/11, Iran is re-emerging as a regional power. Just as Iran resurges, tensions between it and the West have risen sharply. The bone of contention—Iran's nuclear program—has quickly mushroomed into *the* Middle East issue with the whole of the Western world convinced that Iran poses a serious threat should it go nuclear. Still others cry hypocrisy, in light of the sanctimony of regional and global nuclear powers.

## The World Is Misinformed About Iran's Nuclear Program

To add insult to injury, the shocking comments of Iran's President concerning the wiping of another sovereign (Israel) off the map, his questioning of [the] Holocaust, or calling 9/11 [2001 terrorist attacks] a "suspect event," have done little to defuse the growing Western unease with Iran's nuclear program. In the same vein of tactless statesmanship, recently the Israeli cabinet Minister, Rafi Eitan, suggested his country could kidnap the Iranian President, naturally causing outrage amongst the Iranians, while the former U.S. Presidential hopeful, Senator Hillary Clinton, in a not so distant interview with ABC's *Good Morning America*, openly declared if she was president she would "totally obliterate" the Iranians if they "consider" launching an attack on Israel. This threat comes on the heels of repeated refusals by the United States to rule out nuclear first strikes against Iran; declarations in direct violation of the U.S. Negative Security Assurance pledge to not use nuclear weapons against non-nuclear armed members of the nuclear Non-Proliferation Treaty (NPT), as is the case with Iran. Such threats are equally in contravention of *International Court of Justice advisory opinion on the Legality of the Threat or Use of Nuclear Weapons* (1996), as well as [United Nations] Security Council Resolution 984. Such reckless fighting words from all sides only serve to aggravate a hyped up, irrational race towards war.

Sensibly to date, the Security Council has maintained diplomacy will be the *modus operandi* ["mode of operation"] in dealing with Iran. However, how will diplomacy prevail when the current debate surrounding Iran's nuclear program is misinformed, chiefly dominated by one version of the discourse? . . .

### Iran's Nuclear Power Needs Are Legitimate

The genesis of Iran's nuclear program can be traced to the 1950s, when the country began flirting with the idea of developing nuclear energy. Iran's nuclear program was conceived with enthusiastic help from the United States, as well as European governments, notably France and Germany. Iran ratified the NPT in 1970, bringing its program under the inspection regime of the International Atomic Energy Agency (IAEA). Iran has equally ratified other treaties which proscribe the development and use of WMDs [weapons of mass destruction].

The 1979 Revolution, which toppled the Iranian monarchy, brought an abrupt end to Western support of Iran's nuclear program and the Iran-Iraq war, which started a year after, virtually closed the door to further cooperation. The program was later revived without Western assistance.

While the political climate in Iran is vastly different, the position of Iranian governments both pre- and post-Revolution concerning

*An interior view of the Bushehr nuclear power station in Iran is shown here. In the 1950s, with assistance from the United States, France, and Germany, Iran developed its nuclear program for use as an energy source.*

the country's need and inalienable right to nuclear technology has not changed. Iran has *always* maintained its need for nuclear power as an alternative source of energy to supply its booming population (some 70 million) and rapid industrialization. It is estimated, at current rates of production, the country's oil reserves will be depleted within decades. From the times of the last Iranian monarch to the present, Iran's position is that its valuable yet finite oil resources should be used for high-value products and not wasted on generating electricity. This is not a conveniently packaged reason offered by Iran. At the inception of the program, the Gerald Ford Administration gave credence to this claim. The Ford strategy paper at the time stated that: "introduction of nuclear power will both provide for the growing needs of Iran's economy and free remaining oil reserves for export or conversion to petrochemicals"; an assessment later echoed by others, including the U.S. National Academy of Sciences, and the Foreign Affairs Select Committee of the British Parliament.

## Iran Has Every Right to Develop Nuclear Energy

Many important details of Iran's nuclear program simply do not form part of the mainstream debate. Contrary to the myth surrounding Iran's nuclear program, an informed and *reasonable* observer will quickly realize there are indeed two sides to every coin, and that claims of the Iranian nuclear "threat" are arguably more political than factual; that the United States' unbending stance in rejecting Iran's offer of negotiations without preconditions—the United States insists uranium enrichment must be totally suspended—has served to exacerbate a dire situation. The fact is, Iran is in compliance with international law in practicing its legitimate right to develop nuclear energy technology in accordance with the NPT. Let us explore some additional facts.

## Iran Is in Compliance with International Law

First, Iran informed IAEA of its plans to resume its nuclear program. The latter offered assistance in producing enriched uranium under its Technological Assistance Program. Second, article IV of NPT affords an inalienable right to signatory nations to nuclear technology "for peaceful purposes." Demanding Iran—a signatory of the treaty—to suspend enrichment without *credible* evidence it is developing nuclear weapons is, in essence, a violation of Article IV. In law, Iran is under no obligation to negotiate so long as it does not deviate from the "peaceful purposes" test—under international pressure it is negotiating as a confidence building measure. Third, the IAEA, whose detective work in the field is more accurate than "remote detection" highly relied on by intelligence services, has conducted countless on-site inspections on Iran's nuclear sites—by 2005 alone, 1200 person/days of intrusive

> **FAST FACT**
>
> The Energy Information Administration reports that the United States has the most nuclear reactors in the world.

# U.S. Policy Toward Iran

A 2008 poll of America's top foreign policy experts revealed the majority believe American leaders do not know how to deal with Iran.

## How has U.S. policy toward Iran advanced U.S. national security goals?

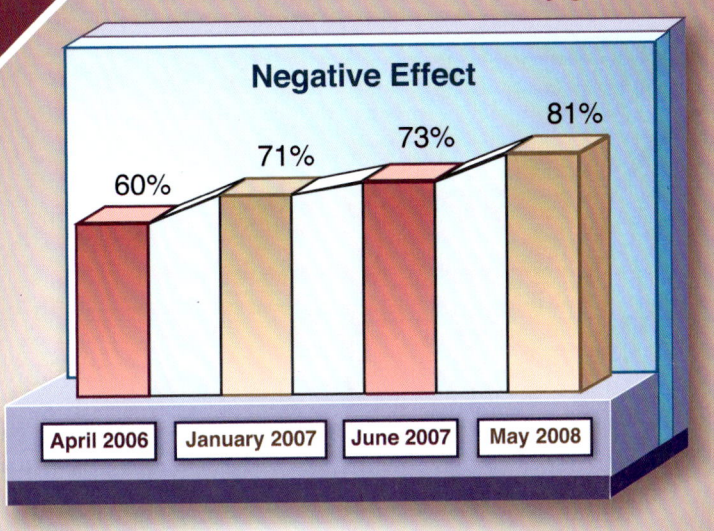

**Negative Effect**

| April 2006 | January 2007 | June 2007 | May 2008 |
|---|---|---|---|
| 60% | 71% | 73% | 81% |

## Is it likely that Iran would transfer nuclear weapons to terrorists?

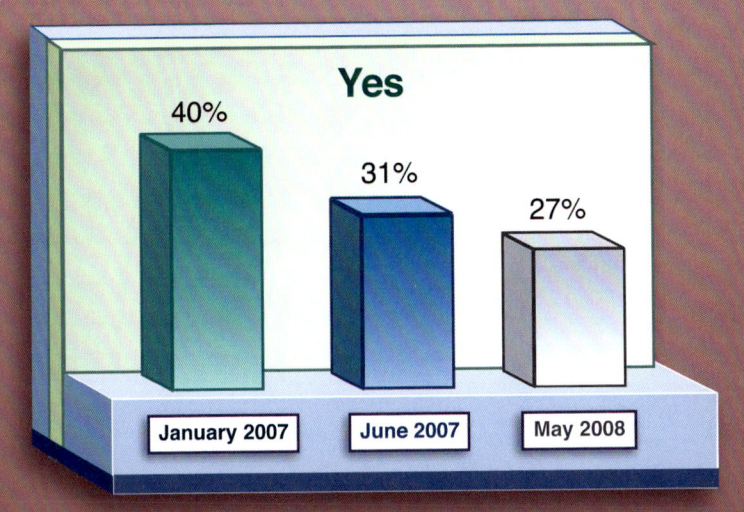

**Yes**

| January 2007 | June 2007 | May 2008 |
|---|---|---|
| 40% | 31% | 27% |

Taken from: *Foreign Policy*, "The Terrorism Index," September/October 2008, p. 82.

inspection were carried out—and while it has reported on technical compliance failures, it has not produced a scintilla of evidence suggesting Iran's nuclear program is other than for civilian purposes. Fourth, the IAEA has repeatedly confirmed Iran's nuclear program "remains in peaceful use."

Fifth, Iran has met its obligations under the NPT, and when issues have arisen, responded with remedial steps. Sixth, Iran *proprio motu*[1] implemented the IAEA Additional Protocol and offered to entertain more rigorous transparency measures, bringing its program under a most strict inspection regime. Iran's referral to the Security Council in 2006 brought an end to such initiatives, and its full cooperation with the IAEA has since suffered as a result. Seventh, Iran has granted unprecedented concessions and invited Western countries to become partners in its uranium enrichment program as further transparency measures.

Eighth, Iran has offered to renounce plutonium extraction technology, negating its capacity to build nuclear bombs. Ninth, Ayatollah Ali Khamenei, Iran's supreme leader and head of the armed forces, has repeatedly declared Iran will not attack any country, issuing a "fatwa"/ban against the production and use of nuclear weapons—calling for a nuclear weapons free Middle East. Let it not be mistaken, aside from the fact that a nuclear arms race in the Middle East will work to the detriment of Iranian interests, the country is equally under no illusion that it can ever compete in a nuclear war in view of the superior technology and arsenal of other regional and world nuclear powers. Tenth and finally, the IAEA has condemned the United States over reports issued by a congressional committee convened on Iran's nuclear program, calling its contents "erroneous and misleading."

## Iran Should Be Allowed to Develop Nuclear Power

As evidenced from the above, the picture is not as black and white as one would, otherwise, be inclined to believe. From the Iranian authorities' outlook, the current row has little to do with a genuine international attempt at maintaining peace and security; rather it is a political game of double-standards and "nuclear and scientific apartheid," where Iran is being forced to forfeit its [in]alienable right to peaceful nuclear energy.

---

1. A legal term meaning to act on one's own initiative.

**EVALUATING THE AUTHORS' ARGUMENTS:**

Other authors in this chapter have claimed that Iran does not need to develop nuclear power because it has large oil and gas reserves. How does Shoamanesh respond to this claim? With which position do you agree? Why?

# Chapter 3

# How Should the United States Deal with Iran?

*Well-staffed antiaircraft emplacements surrounding the Iranian nuclear power plant at Bushehr are evidence of Iran's determination to have a nuclear power program.*

## Viewpoint 1

# The United States Should Consider Declaring War on Iran

## Peter Brookes

*"Keeping the military option on the table for dealing with the Mullahs of Mayhem's atomic intransigence makes good policy sense."*

The United States should consider declaring war on Iran if it wants to stop the country from developing nuclear weapons, Peter Brookes argues in the following viewpoint. He warns that Iran may already have as many as seventy nuclear-related sites hidden across the country. At these sites, Brookes says, Iran is developing weapons of mass destruction. If allowed to continue its nuclear program, Brookes warns Iran could launch deadly nuclear attacks on the United States and its allies in the very near future. Diplomacy and economic sanctions have shown little success in stopping Iran from developing its nuclear weapons capabilities. This is why, Brookes says, the United States should threaten war against Iran. It is only the threat of war that will force Iran's leaders to halt their nuclear pursuits. The author concludes that destroying

Peter Brookes, "Iran: Our Military Options," The Heritage Foundation, January 23, 2006. Reproduced by permission of The Heritage Foundation.

Iran's nuclear sites might be the only way to safeguard the world from this threatening rogue nation.

Brookes is a senior fellow at the Heritage Foundation, a public policy research institute that promotes conservative public policies. He is also the author of *A Devil's Triangle: Terrorism, WMD and Rogue States.*

**AS YOU READ, CONSIDER THE FOLLOWING QUESTIONS:**
1. According to Brookes, a minimum of how many nuclear-related sites are scattered across Iran?
2. What three key nuclear sites does the author say the United States could strike by air?
3. How does Brookes say Iran might respond if the United States attacked it?

A reporter last month, [December 2005] asked Lt. Gen. Dan Halutz, the Israel Defense Force's chief of staff, how far Israel is willing to go to stop Iran's nuclear (weapons) program; the general answered: "2,000 kilometers"—the flying distance from Israel to Iran's key nuclear sites.

Keeping the military option on the table for dealing with the Mullahs of Mayhem's atomic intransigence makes good policy sense. Diplomacy and "soft power" options such as economic sanctions are always more effective when backed up by the credible threat of force.

### Iran's Nuclear Sites Are Hidden

Unfortunately, flattening Iran's nuclear infrastructure isn't easy or risk-free—and could have serious consequences for American interests. The key challenge: the program is underground—literally and figuratively.

Iran burrowed many [nuclear] sites deep below the soil, making them much tougher targets. (It also put some near populated areas to make civilian casualties a certainty if attacked.) And these are the sites we know about: *At least* two dozen nuclear-related sites are scattered across the country (which is four times California's size)—but it may be more than 70.

By burying and dispersing its facilities, Iran is clearly trying to avoid the fate of Saddam Hussein's nuclear program back in 1981—when

Israeli F-16 fighters, crossing Jordan and Saudi Arabia, destroyed Iraq's 40-megawatt Osiraq reactor in a dawn raid, effectively setting Saddam's nuke dreams back a decade.

An Israeli strike at Iran today [2006] might feature fighters carrying satellite-guided JDAM bombs, cruise missiles on diesel subs—and Special Forces. But the task would be *much* tougher than the Osiraq strike, thanks to the number of targets and their dispersion, and the greater distances from any Israeli base.

## A U.S. Attack on Iran Would Debilitate Its Nuclear Program

What about *U.S.* airstrikes? These could take a range of forms, depending on policymakers' desires. Surgical strikes might limit their targets to Iran's air defenses (for access) and key nuclear sites (e.g., Bushehr,

*This satellite photo shows that Iran may be placing nuclear sites inside special tunnels, which will make them harder to strike in a military action.*

How Should the United States Deal with Iran? 95

Natanz, Arak). Or an escalated attack could nail all suspected nuke facilities—*plus* forces Tehran might use in a counterattack, such as its ballistic missiles and conventional forces.

Depending on the strike's objective, think Operation Iraqi Freedom: B-2 stealth bombers carrying bunker-busters, F-117 stealth fighters and other Navy/Air Force strike assets from carriers and theater bases—plus Navy destroyers and subs loosing cruise missiles on Iranian targets.

> **FAST FACT**
>
> According to U.S. military officials, five Iranian boats made hostile moves toward U.S. ships entering the Persian Gulf in the winter of 2008.

But could a raid destroy all sites? Thanks to the covert nature of the Iranian program, that's not clear. It's highly likely, though, that striking key facilities would set the program back, *possibly* causing [Iranian capital] Tehran to reconsider the folly of its proliferation perfidy.

## Iran Is Likely to Retaliate After a U.S. Attack

But it's unlikely to be that simple. After an assault, Iran might lash out with a vengeance. We'd have to be fully prepared for some nasty blowback.

Tehran and its terrorist toadies can brew up some serious trouble for both America and Israel—or anyone else that supported an attack on the fundamentalist Islamic state.

The Iranian regime is already up to its neck in the insurgencies in Iraq and Afghanistan. It could certainly increase its financial/material support to the Sunni insurgents, Shia militants, al Qaeda, and the Taliban to destabilize the new Baghdad and Kabul governments—and kill Coalition forces.

And don't forget about Iran's other "secret" weapon—oil. As the world's No. 4 oil exporter, Tehran could rattle oil markets and major economies (e.g., Japan, South Korea, France, Italy) by slashing output. It could also mess with other nations' oil exports—attacking tankers in the [Persian] Gulf using mines, subs, patrol boats or anti-ship missiles.

## The Stakes Are High

The mullahs [religious leaders] could unleash their terrorist attack dogs Hezbollah, Hamas and Palestinian Islamic Jihad against Israel, killing untold numbers in suicide attacks—and scuttling any peace process prospects. Iran could also pound populous Tel Aviv with its *Shabab* missiles mated with chemical/biological warheads.

The U.S. homefront could get hit, too. Over the last few years, the FBI has evicted Iranian intel officers for surveilling New York City tourist/transport sites. Hezbollah has supporters—and likely has operatives—in America who might undertake acts of terrorism or sabotage U.S. ports or bases, too.

Iran now harbors at least 25 senior al Qaeda operatives, including senior military commander Saif al Adel and three of Osama bin Laden's sons. If we come to blows, would Tehran help al Qaeda hit the U.S. homeland? (The offices of Iran's U.N. mission might facilitate such an attack. . . .)

## We Have to Keep War an Option

This doesn't mean we shouldn't use military might to interrupt or end Iran's nuclear gambit; it may be the best/only option. There are no easy answers, only tough choices.

But the military option has to stay on the table. Otherwise, it's a snap that Iranian President Mahmoud Ahmadinejad will let Tehran's nuclear genie out of the bottle.

---

**EVALUATING THE AUTHORS' ARGUMENTS:**

Both Peter Brookes and Stephen Zunes (author of the next viewpoint) agree that Iran would retaliate if the United States attacked it. Describe what each author says Iran's retaliation would look like. What do they agree on? What do they disagree on?

Viewpoint 2

# The United States Should Not Consider Declaring War on Iran

## Stephen Zunes

*"Given the disastrous results of the U.S. invasion of Iraq, a full-scale ground invasion of Iran is out of the question."*

In the following viewpoint Stephen Zunes argues that the United States should not declare war on Iran. In his opinion, Iran's nuclear weapons program and its ability to launch an attack against the United States have been greatly exaggerated. He says evidence indicates it will be years before Iran will be capable of launching a nuclear missile—therefore, it is not an immediate threat. Furthermore, Zunes says, if Iran is threatened with war, it might preemptively launch missiles and torpedoes at U.S. Navy ships in the Persian Gulf. Or, Iranian-backed militias in Iraq could decide to attack American troops. Zunes warns that a lengthy and massive military campaign would ensue, threatening the lives of America's military forces. Instead, Zunes believes the United States should use diplomacy to negotiate a settlement with

Stephen Zunes, "The Iranian Nuclear Threat: Myth and Reality," *Tikkun*, vol. 22, January/February, 2007, pp. 29–32. Copyright © 2007 Institute for Labor and Mental Health. Reproduced by permission of *Tikkun: A Bimonthly Jewish Critique of Politics, Culture & Society.*

Iran—this would save lives and offer a better chance at halting Iran's nuclear program. Zunes concludes that war is not the answer and the focus should be on establishing a planet free of nuclear weapons.

Zunes is a professor of politics at the University of San Francisco. He serves on the advisory board of the Tikkun Community, an interfaith community dedicated to achieving social justice, sound ecological practices, and world peace. Zunes is also the author of *Tinderbox: U.S. Middle East Policy and the Roots of Terrorism.*

**AS YOU READ, CONSIDER THE FOLLOWING QUESTIONS:**
1. According to Zunes, in what year is Iran likely to have a deployable nuclear warhead?
2. What four factors does Zunes predict will cause a U.S. invasion of Iran to fail?
3. What country does Zunes say in 2003 was convinced to give up its weapons of mass destruction diplomatically?

There is a frightening sense of deja vu: Talk of the United States using military force against a Middle Eastern state with a nuclear program that allegedly poses a threat to the U.S. and the global community, and which also happens to sit on one of the world's largest reserves of oil.

Unlike Iraq in 2003, however, Iran really does have a nuclear program. While there is no evidence to suggest that Iran intends to use nuclear technology for purposes other than peaceful applications, concerns that the current civilian program could be a cover for a nuclear weapons development are not unfounded. Underlying these apprehensions is the fact that nuclear power is an unnecessarily expensive and dangerous means of electrical generation for any country, particularly one that is well endowed with other energy resources.

## Iran Unlikely to Have Deployable Nuclear Weapons

However, developing nuclear power for civilian purposes is legal under the Nuclear Nonproliferation Treaty (NPT), which has been signed and ratified by Iran, the United States, and all but a handful of the world's nations. Iran is currently not doing anything that goes beyond what dozens of other signatories of the NPT are doing legally. Nevertheless, the United Nations' [UN] International Atomic Energy Agency (IAEA) has determined that Iran, by failing to report nuclear research activities back in the 1990s, had forfeited many of the rights afforded to other nations in regard to its nuclear development, such as enriching uranium—a restriction that Iran has rejected and has been violating [since 2006].

More than likely, Iran has not yet mastered the technique for turning uranium into uranium gas, which is necessary to reproduce highly enriched uranium. In addition, Iran does not have nearly enough centrifuges to enrich the uranium, either for fuel rods or for weapons, nor has Iran demonstrated the ability to operate cascades of centrifuges on a large scale. Finally, there is no evidence that Iran has developed a design of a missile re-entry vehicle that could carry a nuclear warhead. Indeed, Iran is unlikely to have a single deployable nuclear warhead until at least the year 2015. . . .

Even if Iran aspires to build nuclear weapons, it would be a mistake to assume that the Islamic Republic would use them for aggressive designs. Indeed, the Iranians may have good reasons to desire a nuclear deterrent. . . .

## Iran Should Not Be Invaded

Given the disastrous results of the U.S. invasion of Iraq, a full-scale ground invasion of Iran is out of the question: Iran is three times the size and population of Iraq, the terrain is far more mountainous, the people are more united against foreign attack, and—unlike Iraq in 2003—no sanctions have been in place preventing the country from maintaining and strengthening its military arsenal.

Instead, a broad consensus of military analysts and those familiar with Pentagon planning envision a massive air attack, likely in conjunction with the Israelis, targeting research, development support, and training centers for Iran's nuclear and missile programs, with the aim of killing as many technically competent Iranians as possible. To enhance the likelihood of such a successful aerial assault, there would also be attacks aimed at the comprehensive destruction of Iranian air defense capabilities and command and control centers.

"US Warns Iran," cartoon by Jimmy Margulies, *The Record* of Hackensack, N.J., June 24, 2008, Political Cartoons.com. Copyright © 2008 Jimmy Margulies, *The Record* of Hackensack, N.J., and PolitcalCartoons.com. All rights reserved.

## Iran Would Retaliate If Attacked

Iran would immediately retaliate in a number of possible ways. For example, U.S. Navy ships in the Persian Gulf could become easy targets for Iranian missiles and torpedoes. To counter the possibility of an Iranian attack, the U.S. assault would presumably include pre-emptive attacks against Iranian naval facilities, though this would unlikely be enough to prevent damage to American vessels.

Perhaps a more dire concern would be the situation in Iraq, where American troops are currently operating against the Sunni-led insurgency alongside Iranian-backed pro-government militias. If these militias decided to turn their guns on American forces, the United States would be caught in a vise between both sides in the country's simmering civil war. It can be anticipated that the U.S. would strike Iranian Revolutionary Guards near the Iraqi border, but given how thoroughly infiltrated various Iraqi police and military units are with pro-Iranian elements, there is little the U.S. could do to protect American forces.

The initial phase of a potential air war would continue for days if not weeks, and, assuming some sort of Iranian retaliation, would

*This still from a U.S. Navy video shows Iranian speedboats harassing U.S. Navy vessels in the Persian Gulf. The author says that any attack on Iran will cause the Iranians to attack shipping vessels in the Persian Gulf.*

almost certainly turn into a protracted military confrontation. In other words, this would not be a single series of strikes against a single facility—like the 1981 Israeli attack against the Osirak nuclear facility in Iraq—which would be over in a matter of hours; this would be a massive and lengthy military operation.

## An Attack Would Encourage Iran to Develop Nuclear Weapons

A U.S./Israeli attack on Iran's nuclear facilities would not only be contrary to international law—further enflaming international public opinion against the United States and Israel—it would be very unlikely to succeed in ending Iran's nuclear ambitions. Many of the facilities are deep underground and dispersed over a wide area, making them difficult to eliminate through conventional weapons. Prior to the midterm elections in November 2006, the Bush administration was seriously considering a first-strike nuclear attack, particularly at the nuclear facilities in Natanz and Isfahan.

In any case, there is almost certainly some redundancy in the current Iranian nuclear program that would enable Iran to reconstruct its program in case of an attack. In addition, if Iran's nuclear facilities were raided, the Iranians would presumably formally announce its withdrawal from the NPT and begin a crash program for nuclear weapons development in a more irrepressible manner.

Such an attack would also be a major setback for the growing pro-democracy movement in Iran. The vast majority of Iranians opposed to the Ahmadinejad regime are also united in opposition to U.S. policy and the threat of a U.S.-led attack, a fact that would allow the regime to mobilize the population and crack down even harder on progressive movements.

There are alternatives, however, between going to war and doing nothing.

## A Negotiated Settlement Is Still Possible

It is unlikely that U.S. demands on the United Nations to impose tough sanctions against Iran will be successful. This comes in part because the United States has blocked enforcement of previous UN Security Council resolutions dealing with nuclear nonproliferation when the violators have been allies, such as UNSC resolution 1172, which calls on India and Pakistan to eliminate their nuclear weapons and nuclear-capable missiles, and UNSC resolution 487, which calls on Israel to place its nuclear facilities under the trusteeship of the IAEA. In fact, the United States not only maintains its close strategic relationship with Israel, but the Bush administration has recently agreed to provide Pakistan with sophisticated nuclear-capable jet fighter-bombers and has signed a nuclear cooperation agreement with India.

> **FAST FACT**
>
> A 2006 Pew Research poll conducted in fifteen countries found the majority of people polled in twelve of them felt that the U.S. presence in Iraq was a greater threat to world peace than Iran.

Given that Iran's nuclear weapons ambitions are likely focused on deterrence, a negotiated settlement is still possible. This could eliminate threats of a U.S. attack against Iran and efforts to overthrow its government. Such a diplomatic solution led to an end to Libya's nuclear program in December 2003.

A related initiative could call for the United States to end its opposition to the establishment of a nuclear-weapons-free-zone for the entire Middle East and South Asia, where all nations of the region would be required to give up their nuclear weapons and weapons programs, and open up to strict international inspections. Iran has endorsed the idea, along with Jordan, Syria, Iraq, Egypt, and other countries in the region. Such nuclear-weapons-free-zones already exist for Africa, Central Asia, Southeast Asia, the South Pacific, Antarctica, and Latin America.

### A Nuclear-Free Planet Is the Best Solution

Thus far, however, the Bush administration has rejected such a call, insisting that the United States has the right to decide which countries get to have such weapons and which ones do not, effectively demanding a kind of nuclear apartheid. Not only are such double standards unethical, they are simply unworkable: any effort by America to impose a hierarchy of haves and have-nots in the region would simply fuel rebellion from the have-nots.

The only realistic means of curbing the threat of nuclear proliferation in the Middle East is to establish a law-based, region-wide program for disarmament, by which all countries—regardless of their relations with the United States—must abide.

And, ultimately, the only way to make the world completely safe from the threat of nuclear weapons is for the establishment of a nuclear-free planet, in which the United States—as the largest nuclear power—must take the lead.

---

**EVALUATING THE AUTHORS' ARGUMENTS:**

In this viewpoint Zunes argues that if the United States threatens Iran with war, Iran will likely speed up its nuclear weapons program to protect itself. The author of the previous viewpoint, Peter Brookes, argues that the threat of war will deter Iran from continuing its nuclear program. With which author's perspective do you agree? Why?

# Viewpoint 3

# The United States Should Impose Economic Sanctions on Iran

## Daniel Doron

*"Iran's nuclear project can probably be stopped by significantly cutting its oil income."*

Economic sanctions would deter Iran from developing nuclear weapons, argues Daniel Doron in the following viewpoint. He explains the threat a nuclear Iran would pose to the United States and the international community. As such, the United States must find a way to halt Iran's nuclear program to safeguard itself against a potential attack. Since Iran has not been cooperative thus far, Doron believes the United States should impose economic sanctions on the country's oil industry. These sanctions could include taxing Iran's oil, blocking shipping and loading facilities, or even creating trade barriers. Since Iran's economy depends heavily on the money it gets from selling its oil, its leaders might be willing to stop developing their nuclear

Daniel Doron, "Yes, Iran Can Be Stopped: The Iranian Regime Can't Live Without Its Oil Money," *The Weekly Standard*, February 1, 2007. Reproduced by permission of the author.

program. Doron concludes the best way to change Iran's nuclear policies—and the best way to avoid war—is to impose economic sanctions on Iran.

Doron is president of the Israel Center for Social and Economic Progress, an independent pro-market policy think tank.

**AS YOU READ, CONSIDER THE FOLLOWING QUESTIONS:**
1. According to Doron, what factors have made the Iranian economy so weak? List at least two of them.
2. According to the author, what effect would "plunging Tehran into darkness" have on Iranian leadership?
3. What does the word "petrodollars" mean in the context of the viewpoint?

Iran's nuclear project can probably be stopped by significantly cutting its oil income. A meaningful decline in this main source of Iran's income would force its leadership to choose between butter and guns. This is a critical choice; the ayatollahs cannot hope to maintain their hold on power if they cannot feed the tens of millions of destitute citizens now kept afloat with immense welfare outlays. As long as high oil prices and exports provide them with enough income to finance both their costly welfare program and their ambitious, expensive nuclear project, they can and will do both. If reduced means compel a choice, the survival instinct will force them to choose rice rather than enriched uranium.

So why has so little been done to reduce Iran's oil income? Military and diplomatic experts in the West have not yet considered the full extent of Iran's economic vulnerability. Like the Kremlinologists of yore, whose chief efforts were directed at avoiding a nuclear conflagration between the Soviet Union and the West, those dealing with Iran have become totally enmeshed in diplomatic moves to head off Tehran's nuclear ambitions, ignoring the less obvious but more crucial economic processes that underlie Iran's power. Very few Kremlinologists predicted the implosion of the powerful Soviet empire, an implosion that had far more to do with economics than with diplomatic efforts at containment. The same may be happening now with regards to Iran.

The Iranian economy is in shambles. In an effort to please their lower-class supporters in the wake of the revolution, the ayatollahs slapped price controls on agricultural products. Within several years this resulted in the devastation of what was once a prosperous agricultural sector. Millions of farmers had to leave their farms and move to shanty towns near major urban centers. There they were fed by Islamic charities financed by the confiscated assets of the shah. Charity was allocated by family size. This encouraged higher birth rates and caused a population explosion, more than doubling Iran's population and putting further strain on its welfare system.

Mismanagement and corruption, which are endemic to dictatorial regimes, further increased inflation and unemployment, leaving millions of those inhabiting the politically volatile shanty towns barely able to keep their heads above water. Should a cut in oil income force the government to cut back on its welfare subsidies, it will risk a massive revolt—this time not by disgruntled students, who can be marginalized and brutally suppressed, but by the very Islamic masses that have been supporting the revolution as long as it secured their livelihood and lifted their morale with the promises of a victorious jihad.

> **FAST FACT**
> According to the U.S. National Foreign Trade Council, lifting U.S. sanctions against Iran would inject $61 billion into that country's economy and increase its gross domestic product by 32 percent.

If not for ever-higher income from oil, Iran's inefficient and corrupt economy would have collapsed long ago. But with Western complicity, the Iranians have cleverly managed to increase their income. By inflaming the Arab-Israeli conflict and supporting terrorism, they also foment tension that leads to higher oil prices. Their investment in Hezbollah, you might say, has really paid off.

Even a partially successful effort to reduce Iran's income from oil could have great impact, because there are already signs of breakdown in the Iranian economy. In a January 10 *Jerusalem Post* piece, "Ahmadinejad's Reign Threatened by Soaring Housing Prices,"

*The author points to a sagging Iranian economy that is vulnerable to economic sanctions as being the best deterrent to Iran's nuclear weapons ambitions.*

Meir Javedanfar, an independent analyst, is quoted to the effect that 800,000 new families are formed in Iran annually but only around 450,000 housing units are constructed. Prices of apartments in some parts of Tehran have increased by 3,000 percent since 1990. There were 2 million applicants for 30,000 housing loans offered by the government. "The main reason people voted for Ahmadinejad," Javedanfar concludes, "was because of internal problems such as corruption, inflation, housing and unemployment. . . . Unless he confronts these issues, in the next elections his position would be in danger."

Recently, 150 lawmakers, at the core of the Iranian establishment, signed a letter criticizing Ahmadinejad "for policies that led to a surge in inflation." These lawmakers linked their criticism of economic policy to a misguided nuclear policy that may provoke serious international sanctions. A group of powerful businessmen, known as the Islamic Coalition Party has also called for moderation in the country's nuclear policies to prevent further damage to the economy.

A Western-induced cut in oil income can greatly accelerate such political pressures. How could a cut in Iran's oil income be achieved? The U.S. government could of course try to use its enormous clout to bring pressure on firms that trade with Iran or facilitate its financial transactions. It could also put pressure on the Iranian currency. Admittedly such steps are complicated and may not be sufficient. But why not try?

Then there is the possibility of sanctions aimed directly at Iran's oil export industry. Both proponents and opponents of sanctions tend to warn how difficult and complicated a successful oil embargo would prove, since it would be resisted by some shippers, notably by the two nations that constantly strive to undermine Western interests, Russia and China.

But an embargo need not be perfect to achieve its goals, since it is sufficient to reduce Iran's oil income markedly, not cut it off entirely. This could be accomplished by blockading the few major Iranian loading facilities—a much simpler task than blocking ships on the high sea.

If more stringent economic sanctions fail to deter Iran's nuclear ambitions, one can always consider militarist steps, but more graduated and finely honed than are usually suggested. Opponents of military pressure on Iran claim that it would be futile because no military measures could give us confidence of successfully neutralizing the entire Iranian nuclear undertaking. Much of it, they explain, is buried underground and may be so thoroughly protected as to escape damage even from a nuclear strike.

But it is not really necessary to destroy the Iranian program down to the last centrifuge in order to effectively stop it. If serious damage can be inflicted on the electrical grid and on fuel depots and transmission facilities, such damage could effectively stop nuclear production. Even where independent electrical generation facilities are housed in underground silos, their fuel supply will eventually dry up. More important, plunging Tehran into darkness in a way that will not only cripple the government and its command and control centers but will make civilian life unbearable may be more than enough to return the Iranian leadership to its senses.

Iran seeks a nuclear capability for more reasons than fulfilling its dream of destroying Israel (they know Israel can retaliate, so even if they fervently wanted to destroy it, they might just continue to arm Arab terrorist proxies and have them bear the consequences, as they have done with Hezbollah). Iran needs an atomic weapon to one day take control of the flow and the price of oil, a strategic goal it has pursued since the days of the shah. Once it is in possession of an atomic weapon, it could control the Straits of Hormuz with impunity and dictate a constant, if gradual rise in the price of oil. No one will risk an atomic confrontation, let alone the threat of the Saudi oil fields being incinerated, to prevent a gradual rise in the price of oil.

The Iranians could then secure all the income they need to preserve—and even spread—their revolution. See what Arab petrodollars have done to the immune system of Europe, how they incapacitated it and made it impotent in dealing with growing Islamic radicalism in its midst. An Iranian-induced transfer of wealth caused by a steep rise in the price of oil will dwarf the already dramatic impact that Arab petrodollars have had on European politics and culture.

Pushing the hated West into economic decline will make it so weak politically and militarily that it will be in no position to resist when the time is ripe for the Iranian takeover of Saudi Arabia, its oil fields, and no less importantly in Tehran's eyes, Islam's holiest places. Shiite control of these Holy Places and of the Muslim jihad will finally bring the hated Sunnis, and especially the most hated Wahhabis, under

# A History of U.S.-Iranian Relations

The United States and Iran have a long history of both friendly and hostile periods. Experts hope that negotiations and diplomacy can define future relations between the two countries.

|  |  |
|---|---|
| 1953 | Iranian prime minister Muhammad Mossadeq is overthrown by U.S. and British intelligence services. |
| 1979 | Religious leader Ayatollah Khomeini takes control of Iran, establishing the Islamic Republic. |
| 1979 | Iranian students take sixty-three U.S. embassy workers hostage. The United States severs diplomatic ties and imposes sanctions on Iran. |
| 1981 | The last of the U.S. hostages are freed in January after being held for 444 days. |
| 1995 | President Bill Clinton claims Iran is a sponsor of terrorism and imposes sanctions on it. Iran denies sponsoring terrorism. |
| 2001 | The United States claims Iranian forces were behind the 1996 bombing of an American military base in Saudi Arabia. Iran denies the charges. |
| 2002 | President George W. Bush describes Iran, Iraq, and North Korea as being part of an "axis of evil." |
| 2002 | The United States accuses Iran of trying to develop a secret nuclear weapons program. As proof, it publishes satellite images of two Iranian nuclear sites under construction. |
| 2003 | The United States sends humanitarian aid to Iran after an earthquake in the city of Bam kills up to fifty thousand people. |
| 2004 | The United Nations adopts a resolution condemning Iran for keeping some of its nuclear activities secret. Iran in turn bans inspectors from its sites for several weeks. |
| 2005 | Iranian president Mohammed Khatami vows his country will never give up nuclear technology but claims it is not for military purposes. |
| 2006 | U.S. Secretary of State Condoleezza Rice warns that Iran's nuclear program is the greatest challenge the United States faces. |
| 2007 | The U.S. military accuses Iran of supporting insurgents in Iraq. |
| 2008 | President Bush describes Iran as "the world's leading state sponsor of terrorism." |
| 2009 | President Barack Obama sends a videotape to the people of Iran indicating that he wants to start a new chapter in relations between the two countries "that is honest and grounded in mutual respect." |

Compiled by the editors.

Shiite domination, and fulfill another dream and strategic goal of the Islamic Republic of Iran. Shiite jihad will triumph "peacefully."

This is the strategic calculus we must weigh when assessing the risks and benefits of taking timely action to stop Iran from acquiring a nuclear capability.

> **EVALUATING THE AUTHOR'S ARGUMENTS:**
>
> The author of this viewpoint, Daniel Doron, is the founder of Israel's Shinui Party and president of the Israel Center for Social and Economic Progress. Does it surprise you that the author favors imposing economic sanctions rather than war on Iran, given the volatile relationship between Israel and Iran? Why or why not? Explain your reasoning.

## Viewpoint 4

# The United States Should Initiate Talks with Iran

### Reza Zia-Ebrahimi

*"If the United States is sincere in its wish to see a more moderate regime in Tehran, the best policy would be to ... establish direct negotiation channels."*

In the following viewpoint Reza Zia-Ebrahimi argues that the United States should initiate talks with Iran to convince it to abandon its nuclear weapons program. The author explains that in the past, the United States has threatened Iran with military attacks and oil embargoes if it did not disclose information about its nuclear weapons program. But this tactic has only fueled Iran's sense of nationalism and encouraged it to develop nuclear weapons to keep it safe. Zia-Ebrahimi suggests a better tactic is for the United States to negotiate with Iran. He predicts that Iran is likely to respond positively to diplomatic engagement because it will not feel as vulnerable to a U.S. attack. Zia-Ebrahimi concludes that negotiating with Iran is a moderate course of action and is the best way to avoid war and nuclear attack.

Zia-Ebrahimi is a lawyer, political historian, and Middle East consultant who is currently researching Iranian nationalism and

Reza Zia-Ebrahimi, "Iran: The American Threat," Middle East Institute, March 14, 2008. Reproduced by permission.

security in the Persian Gulf. His peace-building efforts have included work with various international organizations, including Interpeace and the World Economic Forum.

> **AS YOU READ, CONSIDER THE FOLLOWING QUESTIONS:**
> 1. What about Iran's neighbors makes it feel insecure, according to the author?
> 2. What three countries does the author say have been allowed to develop nuclear weapons while Iran has not?
> 3. What episode does the author say made Iranians think it is actually the United States that cannot be reasoned with?

Iranian foreign policy is shaped by two factors: an acute sense of insecurity and a thirst for international recognition. Insecurity is largely the result of the country's immediate geostrategic situation. Indeed Iran's natural habitat—characterized by an abnormally high level of interstate tensions and transnational violence—poses major security challenges to the country's policymakers.

## Iran Is an Insecure Nation

To the east, there is Pakistan, an unstable military dictatorship with nuclear capability, and the failed state of Afghanistan, now home to a hostile American military presence. There is instability to the north with a recently crushed independence struggle in Chechnya, guerrilla warfare in Dagestan, and still unresolved conflicts between Azerbaijan and Armenia, as well as between Georgians and Ossetians. The former superpower Russia seems to be on Iran's side but is ultimately unpredictable and therefore unreliable. Iran's western border is shared with Iraq, with which it fought one of the longest interstate conflicts of the 20th century and which is now also home to an American military presence. Last but not least is a nuclear capable Israel, which boasts the region's most powerful military and regularly calls for the Iranian issue to be dealt with "by any means."

This is not intended to dismiss Iran's responsibility in antagonising some of these nations, particularly Israel. Rather, its purpose is to underscore that the Iranians' sense of insecurity is real and justified.

# The World Wants to Talk to Iran

Support for military action against Iran has fallen in thirteen out of twenty-one countries polled. More people worldwide want to use diplomacy to reach out to Iran.

## Possible Actions UN Security Council Should Take If Iran Continues to Produce Nuclear Fuel

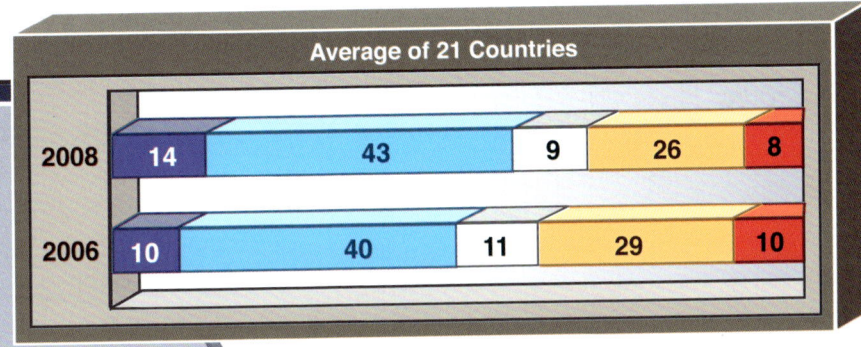

- Not pressure Iran
- Use only diplomatic efforts
- Don't know/Data not available
- Impose economic sanctions
- Authorize military strike

### Average of 21 Countries

| Year | Not pressure Iran | Use only diplomatic efforts | Don't know/Data not available | Impose economic sanctions | Authorize military strike |
|------|-------------------|-----------------------------|------------------------------|---------------------------|---------------------------|
| 2008 | 14 | 43 | 9 | 26 | 8 |
| 2006 | 10 | 40 | 11 | 29 | 10 |

### Participating Countries

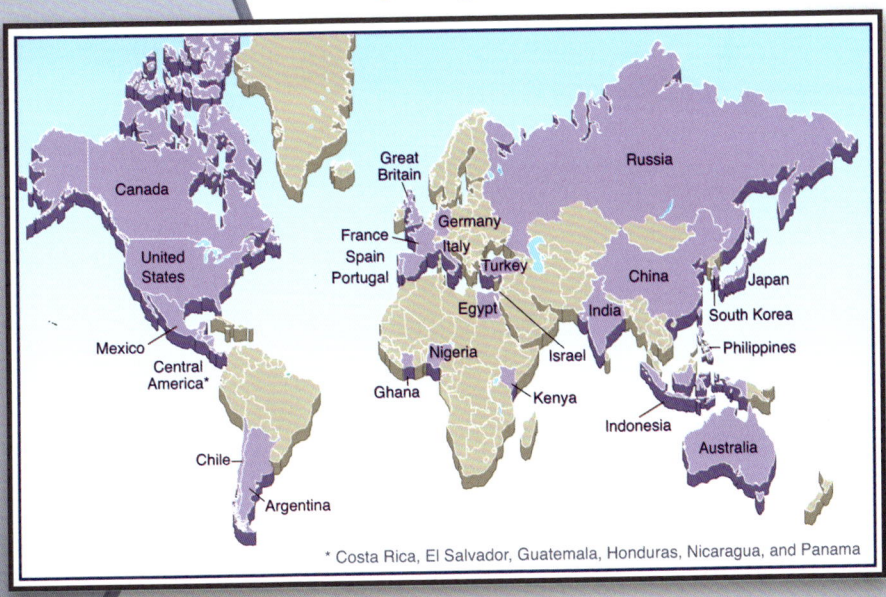

Canada, United States, Mexico, Central America*, Chile, Argentina, Great Britain, France, Spain, Portugal, Germany, Italy, Turkey, Egypt, Nigeria, Ghana, Israel, Kenya, Russia, China, India, Japan, South Korea, Philippines, Indonesia, Australia

*Costa Rica, El Salvador, Guatemala, Honduras, Nicaragua, and Panama

Taken from: BBC World Service, March 11, 2008.

This is especially true when considering that throughout the 20th century Iran has regularly been the object of incursions or invasions (most notably by the Allies in 1941 and Iraq in 1980).

### Iran Yearns for International Recognition

Iran's thirst for recognition is a direct consequence of the country's nationalist posture. This has deep historical roots in past Russo-British interferences into the country's internal political affairs and exploitation of economic resources. After the United States replaced Russia and Britain as Iran's main imperialist challenge, it gave its hand to the removal of democratically-minded Prime Minister Mohammed Mossadeq in 1953 and subsequently supported and armed Mohammad Reza Shah Pahlavi's royal dictatorship.

The significance of this traumatic encounter with the West cannot be sufficiently stressed, and its impact on foreign policy cannot be overstated. It is continuously discussed in public and private circles, effectively reopening old wounds. The most radical form of Iranian nationalism can be understood as a collective post-traumatic condition, which is revived by vivid flashbacks and reinforced by fresh evidence of the outside world's perceived ill-feelings towards Iran.

Iranian nationalism is based on the belief that while Iran is by all standards a powerful country, it is prevented from assuming its place on the world stage by perennial American, British and Israeli opposition. Iran is a populous, culturally sophisticated, nationally cohesive and—by the standards of the developing world—technologically advanced country. How else can a policymaker in Tehran explain why Israel, India and Pakistan have been allowed to develop nuclear arsenals without much international outrage while Iran is ostracized [banished or excluded] for its own program, so far carried out within the framework of the Non-Proliferation Treaty?

> **FAST FACT**
>
> A *USA Today*/Gallup poll conducted in November 2007 found that 73 percent of Americans favored diplomatic efforts in dealing with Iran.

## Iran Has Been Responding, Not Initiating

Iran's pursuit of nuclear weaponry is an obvious response to these concerns. First, it would give Iran some security guarantees and would preclude outside attempts at regime change. Second, the prestige surrounding the possession of nuclear technology is believed in Iran to be a necessary step in the country's quest for international recognition.

With this in mind, it becomes clear why four years of pressure, isolation, subtle threats and serial embargos have so far failed to weaken the Islamic Republic's resolve. They have in fact had the opposite effect by intensifying security concerns and reinforcing the belief that Iran is being denied what its neighbours already possess. The need for a nuclear deterrent is thus rendered even more pressing in the Iranian point of view.

## The United States Should Negotiate with Iran

The alternative to the current trend of threats and embargoes is engagement by the West. This does not come with a guarantee of success but it must be attempted since isolation and non-engagement have been unsuccessful. The 2006 proposal made by the EU 3 (France, Britain

*In his June 4, 2009, speech in Cairo, Egypt, U.S. President Barack Obama reaches out to Muslims worldwide by calling for more negotiations with Iran and other Muslim countries.*

and Germany) gave some vague assurances about regional security schemes and normalisation, which is a start.

However, if viewed from Tehran's perspective it is difficult to believe in Washington's good faith when it still refuses to talk unconditionally to Iran. There was some flesh to former President Mohammad Khatami's opening toward Washington, as it helped provide the Pentagon with crucial intelligence on the Taliban ahead of the invasion of Afghanistan, only to have Iran [along with Iraq and North Korea] included in the "Axis of Evil" [a term used by President George W. Bush] a few weeks later. This episode confirmed the belief among some Iranians that it is Washington that cannot be engaged.

The gradual and infinitely dangerous empowerment of the Islamic Revolution's Guards Corps (IRGC), the impunity with which [Iranian president Mahmoud] Ahmadinejad acts despite his very poor domestic performance, the [return] of hard-line rhetoric, and the new repressive measures against dissidents are all justified using the excuse of an "American threat." If the United States is sincere in its wish to see a more moderate regime in Tehran, the best policy would be to eliminate that pretext and throw all its weight into negotiations over Iran's nuclear file and establish direct negotiation channels. If engagement fails, then the blame can indisputably be laid on Iran's door. But if it succeeds, apart from the tangible benefits of an improved regional security situation, this could also encourage a more moderate Iranian government. History has shown that engagement can moderate.

### EVALUATING THE AUTHOR'S ARGUMENTS:

Zia-Ebrahimi suggests that it is actually the United States that has been unreasonable in its dealings with Iran. Considering what you know about the relationship between the United States and Iran, write a paragraph on whether it is possible that Iran has been misunderstood in the United States. Offer some examples in which the United States could be said to be at fault and some in which Iran could be said to be at fault.

# Facts About Iran

Editor's note: These facts can be used in reports or papers to reinforce or add credibility when making important points or claims.

## The People of Iran
The CIA's *World Factbook* reports the following about the people of Iran:
- As of July 2009, Iran's population was 66,429,284.
- The median age of Iranians is 27 years.
- The average age of men in Iran is 26.8 years.
- The average age of women in Iran is 27.2 years.
- Sixty-eight percent of the population of Iran lives in urban areas.
- The infant mortality rate is 35.78 deaths per 1,000 births.
- Average life expectancy of people living in Iran is 71.14 years.
- Fifty-one percent of Iranians are of Persian descent.
- Twenty-four percent of Iranians are of Azeri descent.
- Eight percent of people living in Iran are Gilaki and Mazandarani.
- Seven percent of Iranians are Kurds.
- Ninety-eight percent of Iranians are Muslim.
- Eighty-nine percent are Shia.
- Nine percent are Sunni.
- Of men in Iran, 83.5 percent are literate.
- Of Iranian women, 70.4 are literate.
- Fifty-eight percent of Iranians speak Farsi.
- Twenty-six percent of Iranians speak in Turkic dialects.
- Nine percent of Iranians speak Kurdish.

According to PBS.org:
- Seventy percent of Iran's population is younger than thirty years old.
- In 2002 women outnumbered men in Iranian universities for the first time.

## Iran's Economy
- According to Djavad Salehi-Isfahani, economics professor at Virginia Tech, 2.3 million of the 3 million unemployed Iranians are under age thirty.

- The Iranian government reports a 2007 unemployment rate of 11 percent.
- Iran's 2007 gross domestic product (GDP) was $852.6 billion.
- Industry made up 45.3 percent of Iran's 2007 GDP.
- Agriculture was responsible for 11 percent of Iran's 2007 GDP.
- Eighteen percent of Iranians lived below the poverty line in 2007.
- Eighty percent of Iran's foreign revenue comes from oil exports, according to a 2008 report by several international financial institutions.
- National Public Radio reports that inflation in Iran is nearing 30 percent.

According to Iranian Trade.org:
- Iran holds nearly 10 percent of world oil reserves.
- Iran has the second largest oil and gas reserves in the world.
- Iran is the Organization of Petroleum Exporting Countries' second largest producer.
- Iran has the world's largest zinc reserves and second largest reserves of copper.

## Iran and Nuclear Technology
- Iran began plans for building a nuclear reactor in Bushehr in 1974.
- The UN Security Council has passed four resolutions demanding Iran halt its uranium enrichment program.

The International Atomic Energy Agency (IAEA) reports the following about Iran's nuclear capabilities:
- Iran has installed three thousand centrifuges to enrich uranium at a nuclear facility in Natanz.
- Three thousand working centrifuges, spinning nonstop for a year, could produce enough weapons-grade, highly enriched uranium for one nuclear bomb.
- Iran had produced 480 kilograms of low-enriched uranium as of August 30, 2008.
- In April 2006 the Iranian parliament passed a resolution calling for Iran to withdraw from the Nuclear Non-proliferation Treaty (NPT).

The United Nations Security Council Resolutions 1737 and 1747 contain the following conditions:
- Iran must cooperate with the IAEA to resolve all outstanding issues related to its nuclear program.
- Iran must verifiably suspend all proliferation-sensitive nuclear activities, including uranium enrichment–related, reprocessing, and heavy water–related activities.
- Iran must grant the IAEA expanded access to information and sites, including at the research and development stage.
- An asset freeze will be imposed on entities and individuals designated by the Security Council or Iran Sanctions Committee for their involvement in Iran's nuclear and missile programs.
- Arms exports from Iran will be banned.
- All states and international financial institutions are called on not to enter into new commitments for financial assistance to the government of Iran, except for humanitarian or developmental purposes.

### The United States and Iran
- A group of Iranian students seized the U.S. embassy in Tehran on November 4, 1979, and held it until January 20, 1981.
- After the September 11, 2001, attacks against the United States, then-Iranian president Mohammad Khatami issued the following statement: "On behalf of the Iranian government and the nation, I condemn the hijacking attempts and terrorist attacks on public centers in American cities which have killed a large number of innocent people."
- President George W. Bush identified Iran as a member of the "axis of evil" in his January 2002 state-of-the-union address.

A July 2008 NBC/*Wall Street Journal* poll found:
- Forty-one percent of Americans support military action against Iran if the country gets close to developing a nuclear weapon.
- Forty-six percent said they would not support military action.

A 2007 CNN/Opinion Research Corporation poll learned:
- Sixty-eight percent of Americans would oppose the United States going to war in Iran.

- Seventy-seven percent of Americans believe the Iranian government is working to develop nuclear weapons.

A January 2009 Gallup poll found that:
- Fifty-six percent of Americans believe the U.S. government should engage in direct diplomacy with Iran.
- Thirty-eight percent believe the United States should not engage in direct diplomacy with Iran.

- A Fox News/Opinion Dynamics poll learned that 80 percent of Americans believe Iran's nuclear program is for military purposes.
- On March 21, 2009, President Barack Obama released a special video message for all those celebrating Nowruz. Translated "New Day," Nowruz marks the arrival of spring and the beginning of the New Year for millions in Iran and other communities around the world.
- Four countries designated by the United States as terrorism sponsors—including Iran and Syria—received $55 million from a U.S.-supported program promoting the peaceful use of nuclear energy, according to a report by Congress's investigative arm.
- General David Petraeus, head of the U.S. Central Command, said in a March 2009 interview on CNN that Iran is "a couple of years" away from having enough highly enriched uranium to make a nuclear weapon.

# Glossary

**ayatollah:** An expert in Islamic jurisprudence, ethics, philosophy, and law. Ayatollah is the highest-ranking title given to clergy leaders in the Shia sect of Islam.

**Ayatollah Ruhollah Khomeini:** The leader of Iran's 1979 Islamic Revolution.

**Bushehr:** Iran's first nuclear power plant. It was expected to be operational in 2009.

**Farsi:** The language spoken in Iran.

**Hamas:** A social, political, and sometimes terrorist organization based in the Gaza Strip, a part of the Palestinian territories. Hamas is believed to receive funding from Iranian sources.

**Hezbollah:** A terrorist group based in Lebanon that is believed to be supported by Iran.

**International Atomic Energy Agency (IAEA):** The international body that regulates nuclear activity. The IAEA has been monitoring Iran's nuclear activity under the suspicion it seeks weapons of mass destruction.

**Islamic Revolution:** The revolution Iran underwent in 1979 that transformed it from a pro-Western nation into a religious theocracy with a strict, repressive social code that follows Islamic law.

**Mahmoud Ahmadinejad:** The current president of Iran. Ahmadinejad has garnered attention for his outlandish anti-American and anti-Israeli statements and actions.

**mullah:** A member of the Islamic clergy.

**Natanz:** An Iranian nuclear facility located between the cities of Isfahan and Kashan. Natanz is Iran's central facility for uranium enrichment. It is believed to have 3,800 operational centrifuges for enriching uranium.

**Persian:** The ethnicity of the majority of Iranians. Although Iran is an Islamic country, Iranians are not Arabs but Persians.

**Shia:** A minority sect of Islam. Iran has the largest Shia population in the world.

**Sunni:** The majority Muslim sect. The populations of most Muslim nations—such as Saudi Arabia and Syria—are Sunni.

**Tehran:** The capital of Iran.

# Organizations to Contact

The editors have compiled the following list of organizations concerned with the issues debated in this book. The descriptions are derived from materials provided by the organizations. All have publications or information available for interested readers. The list was compiled on the date of publication of the present volume; the information provided here may change. Be aware that many organizations take several weeks or longer to respond to queries, so allow as much time as possible.

### American Enterprise Institute (AEI)
1150 Seventeenth St. NW, Washington, DC 20036
(202) 862-5800 or (202) 862-7177
Web site: www.aei.org

The American Enterprise Institute for Public Policy Research is a scholarly research institute that is dedicated to preserving limited government, private enterprise, and a strong foreign policy and national defense. AEI publishes books, including *Democratic Realism: An American Foreign Policy for a Unipolar World* and *The Islamic Paradox: Shiite Clerics, Sunni Fundamentalists, and the Coming of Arab Democracy*, and the bimonthly magazine *American Enterprise*.

### American Jewish Committee (AJC)
PO Box 705, New York, NY 10150
e-mail: pr@ajc.org
Web site: www.ajc.org

AJC works to strengthen U.S.-Israeli relations, build international support for Israel, and support the Israeli-Arab peace process. The committee's numerous publications include the *AJC Journal*, the report *Muslim Anti-Semitism: A Clear and Present Danger*, and the papers "Iran and the Palestinian War Against Israel" and "The Arab Campaign to Destroy Israel."

### American Nuclear Society
555 N. Kensington Ave., La Grange Park, IL 60526
Web site: www.new.ans.org

The American Nuclear Society got started in Washington, D.C., in 1954 to promote the understanding of nuclear science and technology. The organization is made up of one thousand scientists, educators, and other professionals who are committed to unifying those working in nuclear technologies. The American Nuclear Society publishes the journals *Nuclear Science and Engineering, Nuclear News, Fusion Science and Technology,* and *Radwaste Solutions.*

### AMIDEAST
1730 M St. NW, Ste.1100, Washington, DC 20036-4505
e-mail: inquiries@amideast.org
Web site: www.amideast.org

AMIDEAST promotes understanding and cooperation between Americans and the people of the Middle East and North Africa through education and development programs. It publishes a number of books for all age groups, including *Islam: A Primer.*

### The Brookings Institution
1775 Massachusetts Ave. NW, Washington, DC 20036
e-mail: brookinfo@brook.edu
Web site: www.brookings.org

The institution, founded in 1927, is a think tank that conducts research and education in foreign policy, economics, government, and the social sciences. In 2001 it began America's Response to Terrorism, a project that provides briefings and analysis to the public and which is featured on the center's Web site. Its published books include *Iran, Islam, and Democracy.*

### Council on Foreign Relations
58 E. Sixty-eighth St., New York, NY 10021
e-mail: communications@cfr.org
Web site: www.cfr.org

The council researches international aspects of American economic and political policies. Its journal *Foreign Affairs,* published five times a year, provides analysis on global conflicts. Its other publications include "Threats to Democracy: Prevention and Response," and various articles.

## Foundation for Iranian Studies (FIS)
4343 Montgomery Ave., Bethesda, MD 20814
e-mail: fis@fis-iran.org
Web site: www.fis-iran.org

FIS is a nonprofit organization started in 1981 as an educational and research institution. FIS studies and reports on Iranian history, culture, government, and society. FIS publishes the quarterly journal *Iran Nameh*.

## The International Atomic Energy Agency (IAEA)
PO Box 100, Wagramer Strasse 5, A-1400 Vienna, Austria
e-mail: official.mail@iaea.org
Web site: www.iaea.org

The IAEA was established in 1957. The agency works with its members to promote the safe and peaceful use of nuclear technologies. IAEA works to ensure that nuclear power and technology policy making includes safety and security, safeguards and verification, and the promotion of nuclear science.

## International Institute of Islamic Thought (IIIT)
PO Box 669, Herndon, VA 20172
e-mail: iiit@iiit.org
Web site: www.iiit.org

This nonprofit academic research facility promotes and coordinates research and related activities in Islamic philosophy, the humanities, and social sciences. IIIT publishes numerous books in Arabic and English as well as the quarterly *American Journal of Islamic Social Science* and the *Muslim World Book Review*.

## Islamic Supreme Council of America (ISCA)
1400 Sixteenth St. NW, Rm. B112, Washington, DC 20036
e-mail: staff@islamicsupremecouncil.org
Web site: www.islamicsupremecouncil.org

ISCA is a nongovernmental religious organization that promotes Islam in America both by providing practical solutions to American Muslims in integrating Islamic teachings with American culture and by teaching non-Muslims that Islam is a religion of moderation, peace, and tolerance. It strongly condemns Islamic extremism and all forms of terrorism. Its Web site includes statements, commentaries, and reports on terrorism.

### National Iranian American Council (NIAC)
1411 K St. NW, Ste. 600, Washington, DC 20005
Web site: www.niacouncil.org

NIAC is a nonpartisan, nonprofit organization that works to advance the interests of the Iranian American community. NIAC provides resources, knowledge, and tools to Iranian Americans to encourage civic involvement and participation in U.S. legislation.

### Nuclear Energy Institute (NEI)
1776 I St. NW, Ste. 400, Washington, DC 20006-3708
e-mail: media@nei.org
Web site: www.nei.org

NEI is the policy organization for the nuclear energy and technology industry. NEI works both within the United States and globally to form policies that further the use of nuclear technology and energy around the world. Members include more than three hundred corporations in fifteen countries that work together to promote the safe use of nuclear power to generate electricity as well as the relicensing of nuclear power plants currently in operation.

### Women's Forum Against Fundamentalism in Iran (WFAFI)
PO Box 15205, Boston, MA 02215
e-mail: info@wfafi.org
Web site: www.wfafi.org

WFAFI works to promote awareness of the special challenges women face living in Iran. WFAFI seeks to promote public awareness through research projects and outreach programs, as well as policy discussions and analysis.

### World Nuclear Association (WNA)
22a St. James's Square, London, SW1Y 4JH United Kingdom
e-mail: wna@world-nuclear.org
Web site: www.world-nuclear.org/info/info.htm

The WNA is a private international organization committed to the peaceful use of nuclear power. WNA believes nuclear power is a sustainable solution to global energy needs and is interested in furthering nuclear technologies and education. WNA publishes papers on nuclear fuel production, industry economics, trade issues, radiological safety, transporting nuclear materials, decommissioning nuclear power plants, handling radioactive waste, sustainability of nuclear energy, security, and safety. The WNA also publishes the brochure *World Nuclear Association: Vision in Action.*

# For Further Reading

## Books

Abrahamian, Ervand. *A History of Modern Iran.* New York: Cambridge University Press, 2008. Presents a historical overview of Iran and explores how its tumultuous past informs its current political and religious state.

Axworthy, Michael. *A History of Iran: Empire of the Mind.* New York: Basic Books, 2008. Explains Iran's complex history as an empire and how the 1979 religious revolution shaped its national identity.

Baer, Robert. *The Devil We Know: Dealing with the New Iranian Superpower.* New York: Crown, 2008. Outlines three possible options for dealing with Iran.

Bergman, Ronen. *The Secret War with Iran: The 30-Year Clandestine Struggle Against the World's Most Dangerous Terrorist Power.* New York: Free Press, 2008. Makes the case that Iran is the biggest threat to U.S. security.

Evans, Michael D. *Showdown with Nuclear Iran: Radical Islam's Messianic Mission to Destroy Israel and Cripple the United States.* Nashville, TN: Thomas Nelson, 2006. Examines Iran's "divine mission" to bring about the apocalypse by building a nuclear arsenal and engaging the United States and Israel in nuclear war.

Harris, Mark Edward. *Inside Iran.* San Francisco: Chronicle Books, 2008. Criticizes U.S. policies toward Iran and suggests a "selective partnership" between the two nations.

Kinzer, Stephen. *All the Shah's Men: An American Coup and the Roots of Middle East Terror.* Hoboken, NJ: John Wiley and Sons, 2008. Asserts that the American-led coup in Iran in 1953 is to blame for terrorism born out of the region.

Madj, Hooman. *The Ayatollah Begs to Differ: The Paradox of Modern Iran.* New York: Random House, 2008. A portrait of Iranian politics and culture.

Nasr, Vali. *The Shia Revival: How Conflicts with Islam Will Shape the Future.* New York: Norton, 2006. Argues that the Shia peoples in the

Shia Crescent (an area that includes Iran) are gaining strength since the fall of Saddam Hussein.

Parsi, Trita. *Treacherous Alliance: The Secret Dealings of Israel, Iran, and the United States.* New Haven, CT: Yale University Press, 2008. Analyzes the relationship between Israel, Iran, and the United States using historical facts and interviews with high-ranking officials within all three governments.

Pollack, Kenneth. *The Persian Puzzle: The Conflict Between Iran and America.* New York: Random House, 2004. Explores U.S.-Iranian relations over the past fifty years and explains why invading Iran is not a practical option.

## Periodicals and Internet Sources

Afrasiabi, Kaveh L. "Are Iran's Missiles a Threat to Europe?" *San Francisco Chronicle*, May 7, 2007. www.sfgate.com/cgi-bin/article.cgi?file=/chronicle/archive/2007/05/07/EDGUSPL10R1.DTL.

American Israel Public Affairs Committee. "Iran's Support for Terrorism," August 14, 2007. www.aipac.org/Publications/AIPAC AnalysesIssueBriefs/Issue_Brief_Iran_Terror.pdf.

Aslan, Reza. "Misunderstanding Iran," *Nation*, February 28, 2005. www.thenation.com/doc/20050228/aslan.

Batchelor, John. "The Iran Threat: Sinister Summer," *New York Sun*, May 17, 2006. www.nysun.com/opinion/iran-threat-sinister-summer/32878.

BBC News.com. "Country Profile: Iran," March 11, 2009. http://news.bbc.co.uk/1/hi/world/middle_east/country_profiles/790877.stm.

Broad, William J., and David E. Sanger. "Iran Has More Enriched Uranium than Thought," *New York Times*, February 19, 2009. www.nytimes.com/2009/02/20/world/middleeast/20nuke.html?_r=1.

Burns, Robert. "Hillary Clinton Invites Iran to Afghan Talks," *Huffington Post*, March 5, 2009. www.huffingtonpost.com/2009/03/05/hillary-clinton-invites-i_n_172181.html.

Clawson, Patrick, and Michael Jacobson. "The Smarter Way to Target Iran," *Policy Watch*, August 17, 2007. www.washingtoninstitute.org/templateC05.php?CID=2650.

Cornwell, Rupert. "Iran Is a Bigger Threat to the U.S. than the Financial Crisis," *Independent* (London), September 24, 2008. www.independent

.co.uk/opinion/commentators/rupert-cornwell-rupert-cornwell-iran-is-a-bigger-threat-to-the-us-than-the-financial-crisis-940206.html.

Duffy, Michael. "What Would War Look Like?" *Time*, September 25, 2006. www.time.com/time/magazine/article/0,9171,1535817,00.html.

Eskandari-Qajar, M.M. "All Talk, No Nukes," *Santa Barbara (CA) Independent*, vol. 20, no. 2, January 26–February 2, 2006. www.wagingpeace.org/articles/2006/01/26_eskandari_qajar_all_talk_no_nukes.htm.

Fathi, Nazila, and Joel Brinkley. "Atomic Activity Resumes in Iran Amid Warnings," *New York Times*, August 9, 2005. www.nytimes.com/2005/08/09/international/middleeast/09iran.html.

Foundation for Defense of Democracies. "Iran's Continuing Threat," September 22, 2008. www.defenddemocracy.org/index.php?option=com_content&task=view&id=11782311&Itemid=380.

Herman, Arthur. "Getting Serious About Iran: A Military Option," *Commentary*, November 2006. www.commentarymagazine.com/viewarticle.cfm/getting-serious-about-iran-a-military-option-10135?page=all.

Hunter, Robert E. "The Iran Case: Addressing Why Countries Want Nuclear Weapons," *Arms Control Today*, December 2004. www.armscontrol.org/act/2004_12/Hunter.

Kristol, William. "And Now Iran: We Can't Rule Out the Use of Military Force," *Weekly Standard*, January 23, 2006.

Kwiatkowski, Karen. "Can a U.S. War with Iran Be Prevented?" LewRockwell.com, February 16, 2007. www.lewrockwell.com/kwiatkowski/kwiatkowski175.html.

McGovern, Ray. "Hoekstra's Hoax: Hyping Up the Iran 'Threat,'" Antiwar.com, August 20, 2006. www.antiwar.com/mcgovern/?articleid=9609.

Peterson, Scott. "How Iran Would Retaliate If It Comes to War," *Christian Science Monitor*, June 20, 2008. www.csmonitor.com/2008/0620/p07s04-wome.html?page=1.

Pipes, Daniel. "Appease Iran?" *Jerusalem Post*, September 25, 2008. www.danielpipes.org/5912/appease-iran.

Ritter, Scot. "The Big Lie: 'Iran Is a Threat,'" Common Dreams.org, October 8, 2007. www.commondreams.org/archive/2007/10/08/4404.

Ros-Lehtinen, Illeana. "The United States, Israel, and the Iranian Threat: A View from Congress," *Issue Briefs*, vol. 8, no. 11, Jerusalem Center for Public Affairs, September 7, 2008. www.jcpa.org/Templates/ShowPage.asp?DRIT=1&DBID=1&LNGID:1&TMID= 111&FID =442&PID=0&IID=2522&TTL=The_United_States,_Israel,_and_ the_Iranian_ Threat:_A_View_from_Congress.

Saeed, Samier. "Re-evaluating the Iran Threat," *New University*, November 10, 2008. www.newuniversity.org/main/article?slug=re-evaluating_the_iran_threat169.

Salama, Sammy, and Elizabeth Salch. "Iran's Nuclear Impasse: Give Negotiations a Chance," James Martin Center for Nonproliferation Studies, June 2, 2006. http://cns.miis.edu/stories/060602.htm.

Sanger, David E. "U.S. Rejected Aid for Israel on Iranian Nuclear Site," *New York Times*, January 10, 2009. www.nytimes.com/2009/01/11/washington/11iran.html.

Schake, Kori. "Dealing with a Nuclear Iran," *Policy Review*, April/May 2007. www.hoover.org/publications/policyreview/6848072.html.

Sheridan, Greg. "A Threat Bigger than Wall Street," *Australian*, September 27, 2008. www.theaustralian.news.com.au/story/0,25197,24408271-7583,00.html.

Sonenshein, Raphael J. "Iran Nuclear Threat: What to Do?" *JewishJournal*, April 19, 2007. www.jewishjournal.com/opinion/article/iran_nuclear_threat_what_to_do_20070420.

## Web Sites

**Central Intelligence Agency (CIA) World Factbook, "Iran"** (www.cia.gov/library/publications/the-world-factbook/geos/ir.html). The CIA is charged with gathering intelligence for the U.S. government. Its factbook page on Iran provides a comprehensive overview of the country's geography, people, government, economy, communications, transportation, and military. It also addresses problem areas, transnational issues, and world concerns and conflicts.

**Iran Watch** (www.iranwatch.org). Iran Watch was founded by the Wisconsin Project on Nuclear Arms Control. The Wisconsin Project focuses on research and pubic education to stop the use of nuclear weapons, chemical and biological weapons, and long-range missiles. The project operates under the direction of the University of Wisconsin and is a private, nonprofit, nonpartisan foundation based in Washington, D.C.

**Iranian.com** (http://iranian.com). Iranian.com is a community Web site started in New York City in 1995. The site features tabs for Iranian music, arts and literature, photos, news, and events. Iran.com's membership spans the globe but is blocked by most Internet providers in Iran.

**Iranian Cultural and Information Center** (www.persia.org). The Iranian Cultural and Information Center Web site was born out of Stanford University in California. The site was set up to teach visitors about Iran's rich and diverse history, art, food, language, and culture. The site produces an online bulletin that features important Iran-related announcements.

**Presidency of the Islamic Republic of Iran** (www.president.ir/eng). Presidency of the Islamic Republic of Iran is a site based in Tehran that covers the latest news from and about President Mahmoud Ahmadinejad. The site presents statements, opinions, and news about Ahmadinejad. It also provides photos, headlines, speeches, and messages from the president of Iran as well as a searchable news archive.

# Index

## A
Ahmadinejad, Mahmoud, *16, 33, 66,* 97, 118
  Iranian lawmakers' criticism of, 109
  on Israel, 21–22, 31–32
  letter to George W. Bush from, *57,* 58
  majority of Iranians are opposed to, 103
  rhetoric of, 24–25, 54, 85
  threats to U.S. by, 15
  U.S. rhetoric on, 40
American Israel Public Affairs Committee, 76
Artiste, Barry, 8

## B
Bennis, Phyllis, 20
*Bild* (magazine), 34
Bolton, John, 34–35, 70–72
Bronner, Ethan, 31–32
Brookes, Peter, 93
Brookings Institution, 9
Bush, George W., 22, 43, 118
Bushehr nuclear power plant, *10, 87, 92*

## C
Carpenter, Ted Galen, 53
Center for Strategic and International Studies, 34
Central Bank of Iran (Bank Markazi), 82
Central Intelligence Agency (CIA), 21
Chemical weapons, 55
Cheney, Dick, 43, 57
Clinton, Hillary, 86
Cole, Juan, 22, 69
Commission to Assess the Ballistic Missile Threat to the United States, 17
Commission to Assess the Threat to the United States from Electromagnetic Pulse (EMP) Attack, 12
*Country Reports on Terrorism* (U.S. State Department), 23

## D
Department of Energy, U.S. (DOE), 67
Department of State, U.S., 23
Doron, Daniel, 105

## E
Economic sanctions
  benefits of U.S. lifting on Iran, 107
  impacts on Iran, 26, 28
  U.S. should impose on Iran, 105–12

ElBaradei, Mohamed, 68, 72, *73,* 74
Electro-magnetic pulse, 13
Energy Information Administration, 88
EU-3 (U.K., France, and Germany), 117–18
    Iran's agreement with, 67–68

F
Fleitz, Frederick, 70–71, 74, 75
Ford Administration, 87
Franks, Trent, 17–18

G
Gates, Robert, 79
Graham, William, 12–13, 14, 15
Graphite, nuclear grade, 82

H
*Ha'aretz* (newspaper), 41
Hader, Leon, 38
Halevy, Efraim, 41, 42
Halutz, Dan, 94
Hamas, 97, 107
    Ahmadinejad enables, 32
    Iran and, 23
Hezbollah, 43, 51, 54, 55, 110
    Ahmadinejad enables, 32
    Iranian support of, 23
    likely has allies in U.S., 97
Hoekstra, Peter, 72

HonestReporting, 30
Hussein, Saddam, 94

I
International Atomic Energy Agency (IAEA), 24, 67, 88–89
    Iran's cooperation with, 68, 74
    on Iran's nuclear activities, 62, 65
Internet, 8
Iran, Islamic Republic of, 7
    development of nuclear weapons unlikely, 69–75
    does not pose threat to Israel, 38–44
    does not pose threat to U.S., 20–29, *27*
    hostile actions of, 96
    is not likely to help terrorists attack U.S./allies, 53–59, *55*
    is surrounded by unstable nations, 114, 116
    nuclear program of, 61–68, *64, 80–81,* 86, 94–95, *95*
    as threat to Iraq, 45–52
    as threat to Israel, 30–37, *36*
    as threat to U.S., 11–19, *13*
    U.S. and nuclear technology of, 84–91
    U.S. military attack on, 26, 96–97, 101–2
    U.S. should consider declaring war on, 93–97
    U.S. should impose economic sanctions on, 105–12

U.S. should not consider declaring war on, 98–104
U.S. should prevent from getting nuclear technology, 76–83
Iran Counter-Proliferation Act (2007), 79
Iran Sanctions Act (ISA, 1996), 79
Iraq
   Iran poses threat to, 45–52
   Iran's presence in, *47, 48*
   Osiraq reactor, 94–95, 102
   U.S. presence in, 103
Iraq Study Group, 42
Islamic Revolution (1979), 7, 86
Islamic Revolutionary Guard Corps (IRGC), 47, 118
   aid to Kurdish groups by, 50
Israel
   Iran does not pose serious threat to, 38–44
   Iran poses serious threat to, 30–37
   strike on Iraq's Osiraq reactor by, 94–95, 102
   would not survive a nuclear attack, 35–36

## J
Javedanfar, Meir, 109
Jerusalem Center for Public Affairs, 32
*Jerusalem Post* (newspaper), 107
Johnson, Larry, 70

## K
Kennedy, Brian T., 18

Khalaji, Mehdi, 49
Khamenei, Ali Hussein, 47, 58, 90
Khan, A.Q., 63, 65
Khatami, Mohammad, 118
Kheirollahi, Solmaz, 8
Kyl, Jon, 18–19, 40

## L
Lanski, Na'ama, 41
Lewis, Bernard, 72
Libya, 103
Livni, Tzipi, 41

## M
Marcinkowski, Jim, 70
Military budgets, 21
Missile defense system, U.S., 18
Missiles
   Iranian, *36*
   Shahab, 34
   testing by Iran, 12–13
Mossadeq, Mohammed, 116
Music, 8

## N
*New York Times* (newspaper), 22
Nuclear Non-Proliferation Treaty (NPT), 24, 86, 116
   and Iran, 88, 99–100, 102
Nuclear technology
   Iran has a right to develop, 84–91
   for metal/fuel/weapons, *71*
   U.S. should prevent Iran from getting, 76–83
Nuclear Threat Initiative, 76

Nuclear weapons
  Iran is probably developing, 60, 61–68
  Iran is probably not developing, 69–75
  Israeli, 41

**O**
Obama, Barack, 18, *117*
Oil
  Iran's income from, 109
  U.S. policy toward Iran and, 26
Olmert, Ehud, 41
Osiraq reactor (Iraq), 94–95

**P**
Pahlavi, Mohammad Reza Shah, 116
Plutonium, 65
Podhoretz, Norman, 39, 40, 44
Polonium 210, 65
Posen, Barry, 39

**Q**
Al-Qaeda
  Iran could assist in case of U.S. attack, 97
  Iran's cooperation with U.S. against, 56–57
Quds Force, 47, 50
  activity in Iraq by, 49, 51
Qumi, Hassan Kazemi, 50

**R**
Rafsanjani, Ali Akbar Hashemi-, 17, 66

Rice, Condoleezza, 39, 58, 71
Rohani, Hassan, 58
Rood, John, 15
Rubin, Uzi, 33–34
Rumsfeld, Donald, 17, 57, 74

**S**
Al-Sadr, Muqtada, 50
Shoamanesh, S. Sam, 84
Shoja, Amir, 7
Surveys
  on diplomatic relations with Iran, 116
  on Iran and terrorists, *89*
  on threat posed by Iran, *13*
  on UN Security Council on Iran, *115*
  on U.S. policy toward Iran, *89*
  on U.S. presence in Iraq 103

**T**
Tenet, George, 39
*Time* (magazine), 58
*Times of India* (newspaper), 82–83
Timmerman, Kenneth R., 11

**U**
United Arab Emirates (UAE), as hub of illegal shipments to Iran, 82–83
United Nations Security Council, 86
  and Iran, *77,* 78, 103
United States
  history of relations between Iran and, *111*

Iran does not pose threat to, 20–29
Iran is not likely to help terrorists attack, 53–59
Iran poses threat to, 11–19
military budget of, 21
and nuclear-weapons-free zone in Middle East, 103–4
overthrow of Mossadeq by, 116
should consider declaring war on Iran, 93–97
should impose economic sanctions on Iran, 105–12
should initiate talks with Iran, 113–18
should negotiate with Iran, 56
should not declare war on Iran, 43–44, 98–104
should not prevent Iran from obtaining nuclear technology, 84–91
should prevent Iran from obtaining nuclear technology, 76–83
Uranium
enrichment of, 63
Iran lacks sufficient quantities for a bomb, 72–74
U.S. House of Representatives Permanent Select Committee on Intelligence, Subcommittee on Intelligence Policy, 61
U.S. National Foreign Trade Council, 107

W

*Washington Post* (newspaper), 56
*Washington Times* (newspaper), 17
Weitz, Gidi, 41
White, Jeffrey, 45
WMD Commission (Commission on the Intelligence of the United States Regarding Weapons of Mass Destruction), 63

Z

Zia-Ebrahimi, Reza, 113
Zunes, Stephen, 98

# Picture Credits

Maury Aaseng, 13, 27, 36, 48, 55, 64, 71, 80–81, 89, 111, 115
AP Images, 10, 25, 42, 47, 60, 66, 78, 92, 95, 102, 108
Mohammad Kheirkhah/UPI/Landov, 16, 57
Majid Mardanian/UPI/Landov, 33
Zhang Ning/Xinhua/Landov, 117
Reuters/Landov, 73, 87

CURRICULUM COLLECTION

JUV 327.73055 Ir1
Iran

JUL 0 1 2013